MADNESS

HOW ONE MAN CAPTIVATED A NATION AND STARTED A BASKETBALL REVOLUTION

Mike DeLucia

Green-T-Books, Somers, NY

www.booksbymikedelucia.com

Photography: Danielle Petri and Helene Magazine-Fishkin
Hank Luisetti Photograph Bronze: Linda A. Cicero /
Stanford News Service
Illustration: Michael Sluchevsky

Editing, Cover Design and Formatting by:
THE BOOK KHALEESI
www.thebookkhaleesi.com

Special Thanks to Nick Garzillo and Ed Aviles.

CONTENTS

Other Titles by Mike De Lucia

Settling a Score

Boycott the Yankees:
A Call to Action by a Lifelong Yankees Fan

For Mom,
As Dad always says,
"You could search the entire Earth, and there would never
be another one like you."

"Just like my grandfather Luigi Del Bianco was finally recognized as chief carver of Mount Rushmore, it's wonderful that people of a new generation will learn about Hank Luisetti's contributions to the sport of basketball."

~ Lou Del Bianco
Author of Out of Rushmore's Shadow

FOREWORD

SYLVESTER STALLONE HAS as much to do with the res-
urrection of Hank Luisetti as anyone. When Rocky was re-
leased in 1976, I was a sophomore at Monsignor Scanlan High
School in the Bronx, and my life's goal was to become a film
actor. I was bitten by the acting bug in 1973 when Ron
MacFarland, a dynamic teacher at my grade school, put on a
rock and roll musical. Prior to that, when grownups asked
what I wanted to be when I grew up, I'd say doctor, lawyer,
or centerfielder for the New York Yankees.

After high school, I went to Queens College for a year,
dropped out, and enrolled in H.B. Studio acting school in the
summer of '79. I worked as a waiter at night, attended acting
classes during the day, and life was good. However, in 1981,
I made two decisions that dramatically altered my direction:
I got engaged to be married, and I went into my own business—assuming that if I were the boss, I'd have control over
my life. I'd have to quit acting school for a while, but I was
convinced that it would all pay off in the end.

In 1982, I borrowed money from my father to begin building a house for my upcoming nuptials, opting again for control over the unknown whims of a landlord. The intended
short break from acting turned into a few years, and I grew
more and more frustrated as time went on. I realized that the
decisions I made to help my career were responsible for oblit-
erating it.

In 1983 I decided to "Stallone" it. I'd write my own

screenplay and star in it as well. I wouldn't have to invest time going to auditions or traveling to Manhattan for acting classes. I'd just write a film and wouldn't sell it unless I played the leading role. Sounds funny now, but back then, I thought it was a rock-solid plan.

I shared my project with the family at our 2:00 p.m. Sunday dinner ritual. My father snapped his fingers and said he knew the perfect story for me. He read about a Stanford University athlete named Hank Luisetti from the twenties or thirties, who revolutionized basketball. He said, "Before Luisetti, total scores of basketball games were between 20 to 30 points, but this kid invented the layup and scored 50 or 60 points in a game. He was generations ahead of his time." The next weekend I took the 6 train downtown to the New York Public Library on 5th Avenue in Manhattan and began the onerous task of researching a ghost. I flipped through frayed card catalog files, scrolled microfilm, printed photocopies that stammered out of archaic Xerox machines, and worked with librarians to unearth the meager details of this forgotten pioneer.

After months of digging around, I was able to piece together a skeleton of his story. My father had most of the Luisetti facts correct, but his memory hiccupped on Hank's biggest contribution. Hank Luisetti was not the originator of the layup. He perfected the running one-handed shot in an era when basketball dogma preached a stop-set-shoot mentality. Players shot and passed with two hands, and a center jump followed every basket. The game was clunky, rooted in defense, and served mostly to fill the gap between football and baseball season.

Hank Luisetti would change all that by introducing the world to his unorthodox playing style. He also initiated other advancements, such as the behind-the-back dribble, which quickened the game's pace and injected fluidity. After Luisetti's innovations, basketball gained a strong fan base of its own, and this led to the advent of March Madness and the formation of the NBA.

While Hank's court heroics elevated him to celebrity status in the latter part of the 1930s, there was little-to-no information regarding his personal life. This was due in part to a lack of paparazzi, a serious illness he contracted during WWII, and the absence of the NBA. Hank Luisetti, the man who reinvented basketball and even starred as himself in a major motion picture opposite Betty Grable, faded into obscurity. Armed with stacks of photocopies, highlighters, pencils, loose-leaf paper, and a "how to write a screenplay" book, I wove together Hank's achievements with the snippets I garnered of his personal life, into the first draft of The Hank Luisetti Story. That milestone was overshadowed by a personal life filled with the urgencies of home, business, and the addition of children. I learned that the difference between busy and "parent" busy is far and wide.

Hank found its familiar spot at the bottom of my "To Do" list and it remained there for decades.

In 1995, I decided that I had wasted enough time on foolish dreams and childish fantasies. I threw in the towel on my acting career, but opened a small acting school called Limelight Performing Arts Center, because like Rocky in Rocky II, I had to be around it. It was liberating to live without the nagging embodiment of a dream nudging me in its direction. There'd be no fanfare, movie deals, or footprints on the Hollywood Walk of Fame—but I would be fulfilled by teaching and satisfied in the knowledge that I tried my best.

I bought my first computer around that time, and I had an urge to dig out my handwritten screenplay, dust it off, and digitize it for posterity. In 1995, I sold my business and started a new one that failed after nine months. For the first time in my life, I was wrestling with overwhelming debt and the possibility of bankruptcy.

I landed a job that barely paid the bills, but kept the acting school going—as more of a labor of love than anything else. I continued the program until it became clear that the time commitment required to keep it afloat, made it impossible for me to get out of debt. I made the decision to shut it down after the April 2000 production.

A teacher friend came to the show and convinced me to go back to school for a teaching degree. I worked out the logistics, quit my job, began a DJ business, and went to college as an English major. I also took acting and screenwriting courses where I developed another version of The Hank Luisetti Story.

I graduated from Manhattanville College in 2005 with a bachelor's degree in English and a master's degree in education. Even though I absolutely love teaching, being an educator is the most challenging career I have ever had. Unless you're a teacher you will never know this. Motivating adolescents who were ripped from their beds at 6:00 a.m. to discuss Shakespeare, Tennessee Williams, or Homer at 7:25 a.m., is harder than it sounds.

From 2005 to 2009, I worked seven days a week preparing lessons, grading papers, answering parent emails, creating quizzes, tests, essays, and adapting to the ever-changing paradigms of the public education system. Common Core is only a spoke in an enormous wheel of motion. I worked all summer revising the lessons that fizzled during the school year only to cycle back again in September. Taking over the school drama club and directing the musicals added to my workload. I'd all but burnt out in 2012 and resigned my position as theater club advisor.

At this point, The Hank Luisetti Story had become a distant memory. I accepted that all it would ever be is a screenplay I'd written that nobody would ever see.

In 2013, I was inspired to write a baseball-themed screenplay that had been bouncing around in my head for over twenty years. However, just before I was to begin, I switched gears and decided to write Boycott the Yankees: A Call to Action by a Lifelong Yankees Fan. I was outraged that baseball players' greed and ego were desecrating America's favorite pastime. Going to a baseball game was no longer something fans could do as often as they wanted. Obscene ticket prices prevented a family from going to a game on a whim or kids from meeting up to take a train to the Stadium. The irony is that fans are having a hard time affording tickets, when it is they who pay for player salaries and owner profits through cable fees, merchandise, food, and ticket sales. We also make it possible for teams to profit from advertising dollars. Fans have the power, because all they must do is boycott games until owners lower ticket prices. No fans equals no money. Owners capitalize on fans because they are not organized.

Boycott the Yankees was an attempt to organize. I thought it would begin a movement since nearly everyone I spoke to passionately agreed with me. After the book's release, I learned that there's a huge difference between talk and action. The book didn't begin a movement, but it received much publicity. I was interviewed in over a dozen newspapers, podcasts, radio programs—including Curtis Sliwa's Drive at 5, and the nationally televised Fox cable show America's Newsroom. By the time I'd finished Boycott the Yankees, I was ready to resurrect The Hank Luisetti Story as a young adult, historical fiction novel. At that time I was calling it, The Man Who Changed Basketball.

It took thirty-five years to arrive, but Madness, the story's newest title, is here to re-introduce Hank Luisetti to the world.

Looking back on it now, I'm astonished that the desire to tell his story stayed alive in me for over three decades. Perhaps, my stubborn personality was responsible for it, but I'd like to think it was Mr. Luisetti nudging me along every time I became sidetracked.

Ever since Sylvester Stallone inspired me to write a screenplay, hold on to a dream, and see it through till the end… even if it was a million to one shot.

CHAPTER ONE

San Francisco, 1926

Galileo High School Gymnasium

TEN TEENAGED BOYS play basketball in the old style — two big guys planted under the basket and man-to-man defense. Tight cotton tank tops and short satin trunks cling to their bodies like a second skin. Numbers and team names sit in the usual spots with the team name on top of the number. Black high-tops with a white toe and heel act as more of a shoe than a sneaker. A tired red and white scoreboard displays essential fourth-quarter information: **Home 25, Visitors 28.**

Buzzing spectators, pounding feet, and an echoing, thumping basketball beating the court floor, all drum the air of the half-filled gymnasium.

The arena has five tiers of bleachers on either side of the court, and the solid white backboards are ribboned with red stripes outlining the inner rectangle. The gym floor is yellowed by copious coats of shellac. Sweaty boys pass the ball dozens of times, using two hands to either push it off their chests or toss it overhead, until a boy stops, sets, and shoots a two-handed shot. The ball slams off the backboard and zips through the net. Claps pepper the air as the players jog toward the center circle. Once they are in their positions, a ref tosses the ball high between the two centers who slap the game back into action.

Blending into the crowd in his shirt, tie, and tweed vest, a man in his late twenties, Ricardo "Ricky" Durán, stands and cheers. He looks down to his left and smiles warmly at ten-year-old Angelo Luisetti or "Hank," a nickname he earns as a teenager. The boy smiles back, dressed in his Sunday best—shorts, suspenders, and a bow tie.

The young Hank intuitively turns his head to the left, where another boy is picking his nose and staring at him from across the aisle. The boy points at him with his free hand and uses his previously occupied fingers to tug on his mother's dress. The woman gazes at Hank's legs, which are encased in bulky metal braces, then grabs her son's hand and switches seats with him.

Hank looks away as a harsh, jarring buzzer trumpets the end of the game. The hometown Galileo Lions lose to the visiting Lowell High Cardinals, 25-30. Spectators rise and rush the exits.

While driving home, Hank looks up at Ricky. "Thanks for bringing me to the game, Mr. Durán."

Ricky glances at the rearview mirror and then at the boy. "You come to the park every day and help me out. It's the least I could do."

Hank smiles.

"I'd have taken you anyway. You're a good kid, Angelo."

Ricky stops the car before a row of narrow, wood and stucco houses on a steep hill. He stretches into the back seat, retrieves a paper shopping bag, and hands it to the boy. Hank's face lights up when he pulls out a ratty, old, leather basketball.

Ricky sits back against the car door. "New equipment came in today."

"It's mine for keeps?"

Ricky nods and smiles. "Yes, Angelo. It's yours."

Hank's metal-encased legs clank as he leaves the car. "Thanks so much, Mr. Durán. I'll see you tomorrow!"

"See you tomorrow, Angelo."

Hank clumps his way up the wooden steps, opens the front door, and waves energetically to Ricky before disappearing inside.

A second-floor window blind snaps closed as Ricky drives away.

* * *

AT FOUR O' CLOCK the next morning, Hank's father, Stefano, opens his son's bedroom door and gazes at the boy wrapped in blankets, before gently rousing him. Stefano, a man in his early forties, has a thick black mustache and wears an old button-down shirt with thick suspenders attached to baggy work pants. Hank groans and turns over.

Stefano puts his hand on Hank's shoulder and shakes him gingerly. "We gotta go to work."

Getting torn from his dreams, Hank lifts his head, bats his squinting eyes, and asks in a raspy morning voice, "You're taking me to your job?"

"All-a day!" Stefano nods, smiling tenderly. Then, he whispers to himself, "All-a day."

Hank shakes his head quickly as though he suddenly remembers where he is. "What time are we coming home?"

Stefano's smile fades but quickly returns. "C'mon. We gotta go."

An hour later, he drives Hank in a rusty Ford pickup with a wooden railing around the cargo bed. They travel down

Russian Hill, one of the original seven hills of San Francisco. A flock of wild parrots squawk in a large maple tree tucked into a side street, and a network of splintery telephone poles and street lamps feed the growing industry of the bustling city. Trolley car tracks and the cables that follow above snake through cobblestone streets. Hank waves to an old man in a horse-drawn carriage just as the sun rises over Fisherman's Wharf.

They park the truck, and Stefano holds Hank's hand as they walk past rows of small, thin fishing boats, or feluccas as they are called, tied to docks while a raggedy pack of stray dogs scavenge for breakfast. Two men pull a felucca out of the water, and a man with a weather-beaten face spreads a large crab in the air. Hank smiles.

Stefano looks at his son. "That's a big-a one."

Fishing nets, mottled with woven chunks of caulk, lay drying over a railing. As Hank's braces clomp along the pier, a man wearing a shabby cap, smoking a long cigar, and mending a net, eyes Hank's legs. Seagulls squawk overhead, bobbing up and down on salty air currents. A fisherman on a docked boat throws crabs into a holding tank, and another from his crew feeds honking seals in the water near the boat.

"Could we feed them too, Papa?"

"Maybe later,"

Stefano and Hank walk down the street of an outdoor market lined with a cornucopia of fresh seafood displays. Men in baggy work clothes haggle around icy beds of fish. Hank holds his nose as he and Stefano walk.

"Take-a you hand from you nose, Angelo."

Nasally, Hank says, "But it smells like poop in here."

Stefano shoots him a look, and the boy removes his hand but scrunches his nose in an attempt to purify the air.

4

MADNESS

A portly man behind a counter takes a crab from a hanging scale. "Stefano, I have-a beautiful crabs for you. A special price." Noticing Hank, he says, "You bring-a you boy today?"

"Yes. Say hello to Rosario."

Hank is digging his finger into the eye of a red snapper.

"Hey, stop-a that," Stefano says.

Rosario laughs. "That's okay!"

Stefano looks at the crab, purses his lips, and continues past the counter.

"Come-a back later, Stefano. I save-a these special for you!"

Stefano takes Hank's hand and leads him through the street. After a few hours of wrangling, Stefano and Hank load ice-packed crates of seafood onto the truck. They drive about twenty minutes away and park in front of six attached brick storefronts.

Hank asks with a yawn, "Why didn't you buy crabs from that fat man?"

"Because he's a thief," Stefano says, exiting the truck. Then, he grabs his son's hand and speaks with sprightly enthusiasm, "Come with me. I have a big surprise for you!" He leads him past the block letters of Stefano's Fish Market to the next store, which displays a bright new sign, Angelo's Frutti Di Mare Ristorante, written in a soft, elegant script.

Hank looks up and asks, "What happened to Mr. Finn's store?"

A wide smile stretches across Stefano's face. "He's-a move out, and you move in."

Hank's eyebrows rumple and Stefano laughs.

"Don't-a you see the name? This is-a you restaurant. Me, Mama, Nonna, and-a you, all workin' together in-a two places."

Hank scratches his nose.

Stefano beams with misty eyes. "God only give-a me one child, and I want to make-a you life beautiful."

Hank looks down for a beat, then up at Stefano. "Papa, why did God make me with bowed legs?"

"You lucky you have the brace to fix, and don't question God, Angelo."

Looking down again, he says, "But I'm different." Hank looks up and locks eyes with his father.

Stefano softens. "You no different—you special. When the doctors said that you mama and me could have no kids, I said, 'You wrong,' and I prayed-a novena to Maria. Then, you come. My bambino!" He crouches down in front of his son. "I buy the store for you future. I plan everything for you."

Hank smiles. "Can we go inside?"

"After we unload-a the fish." Stefano puts his strong arm around Hank's shoulder, and they walk toward the truck with the sun reflecting off the water in the distance.

"Papa, what time do we go home?"

A full moon lights the way for Stefano, carrying his sleeping boy up the front stairs of their home, past a Blessed Mother statue, and through the front door.

CHAPTER TWO

HANK IS A lone figure at the Spring Valley Playground. The lopsided park is a spattering of puddles on asphalt—its chain-linked perimeter has been doctored by neighborhood kids for unauthorized after-hour activity.

Hank flings a basketball like a discus at the hoop and sings in ten-year-old falsetto tones. "And the fans go wild! Haarr!" He lumbers after the ball. "And Angelo sprints for the loose ball." He picks up the ball and hurls it toward the basket, but it bangs off the support pole and Hank cheers. "He scores again! Haarr!" He raises both fists and plods around in a victory lap.

Ricky Durán chuckles as he switches his metal lunch box to his left hand so he can twist the key in the futile padlock. Ricky comes from a large family that has been living in San Francisco since the first Spaniards arrived in the eighteenth century. He's a talented individual with the uncanny ability to fix or make just about anything, and one of his greatest loves is sports—especially basketball. Family aside, the only thing he loves more than playing sports is coaching them. Ricky is wearing green shorts and a green button-down shirt with a parks department patch stitched above his left pocket.

Hank lights up when he sees Ricky. "Hi, Mr. Durán!"

"Good morning, Angelo. Where were you yesterday?"

"My father bought me a restaurant. I'll be working there sometimes and forever after high school." Hank bounces the basketball with two hands.

"How'd it feel to be a workingman?"

"It smelled, but it was sort of fun. I'd rather be playing basketball, though. I want to be like the boys we saw on Sunday night."

"You can be anything you want to be, Angelo."

His voice raises a notch when he asks, "Anything?"

Ricky crouches down to eye level with the boy. "Anything! And starting in September, I'll be working at the high school as a gym teacher and basketball coach. If you practice hard, you could be my star player in a few years."

"I'll practice every day, Mr. Durán! Every single day!"

Ricky stands and motions for the ball. Hank passes to him.

"In shooting, the ball is held with both hands and shot by pushing off the chest, like so."

As the coach demonstrates, Hank is fixed on the man's every movement.

Ricky continues, saying, "Or underhand from below the waist by flicking the wrist." He holds the ball and demonstrates a few times. "The ball is passed with both hands from either above the head or pushed off the chest, and..." He passes to Hank. The ball bounces off his chest and back to Ricky.

"Hey!"

"Always be alert."

"No fair. I wasn't ready!"

"In basketball, you must always be..." Ricky passes, and this time Hank catches it, "...ready. Good! I can see you're going to be a very good student."

Without looking, Hank passes to Ricky who catches it.

"Very good! While you pass and shoot with two hands, you dribble with one. Practice running and dribbling with your right hand from one end of this court to the other. On your way home or when you walk to the store, bring your ball and dribble using your left hand. After a few weeks of that, mix it all together. Okay?"

Hank beams. "Okay!"

"Good boy! Start from here and shoot when you get to the other end. I'll be back soon. I've got to get things opened up." Ricky passes the ball to Hank and walks away.

Hank's eyes lock onto the hoop at the opposite end of the court. He looks down at his legs, takes a deep breath, and bursts into a heavy trek. The boy lumbers around puddles while clumping his way across the court with the will of a bulldog.

* * *

HE PRACTICES HIS drills, day after day, and the days pile as high as that Russian Hill Street he dribbles up and down for years. Each grueling pass of the hill grows the dense muscle and thick tendons, which are the foundation of Hank's superior all-around play. The boy's legs grow straight and powerful while thoughts of metal braces are buried deep like so many awkward childhood memories that sometimes reemerge as pesky, resident insecurities.

At seventeen, Hank is a strikingly handsome six-foot-three basketball machine, dribbling down the park court and expertly navigating his way around puddles and defenders who cannot keep pace with him. He finds an open shot near the foul line before releasing a two-handed set shot that ricochets through the rim and is stormed by a group of leaping teens. At five foot seven, Eddie Kinsman is solidly built with sandy-colored hair in a permanent buzz cut, which earned him the nickname Fuzz; Mac is five eleven with brown hair and blue eyes; Dabbs is six feet tall with wavy blond hair and a pink birthmark shooting from his right eye like a sunburst; Yang, six foot three, has dark skin and jet black hair; and, at five ten, Mario is built like a linebacker. The group is dressed similarly—caps, tattered corduroys, and home-knitted sweater vests over button-down shirts.

Yang tosses the ball to Hank. "Nice one, Ang."

Hank shakes his head and says, "I really have to go."

Mac, with open palms, says, "Just a few more minutes."

"We said that an hour ago." Hank trots away with his basketball. "I'll see you tomorrow."

The boys plead and motion for him to come back.

Hank is pursued by Eddie Kinsman. "Hey Ang... Wait up!"

Hank, running and dribbling, turns and sees Eddie, then slows his pace. As they jog, they dribble and bounce-pass to one another. They've been performing this ritual for so many years, this routine is as natural as breathing.

Hank asks, "You think its past two o'clock?"

"You know it is."

Hank tightens his face and quickens his pace.

"Why does your family eat dinner in the back of your restaurant every Sunday afternoon at two?"

"It's an Italian tradition."

"The Irish have different traditions. On Sundays, my grandfather comes over after mass, and, as he holds up a shot of whiskey, says in his Irish brogue, "The guineas be eatin' about now while we Irish be havin' our first Jameson's."

They turn a corner. Eddie crosses and moves ahead of Hank who leads Eddie with a pass. Eddie catches it and dribbles at a steady pace until Hank jets ahead and crosses in front of him. Eddie leads Hank with a pass.

MADNESS

"If Italians in Italy eat dinner at lunch, do they eat lunch at breakfast?

"Yeah, they eat pizza every morning."

Eddie cranes his neck toward Hank. "Really? I was only joking."

Hank smiles and shakes his head. Eddie cuts onto the sidewalk, and Hank whips him a pass. Eddie runs up the steps of his cedar-shingled home, raises the ball above his head with both hands, and launches it to Hank who's motoring forward. The ball is slightly ahead of Hank, but he leaps up, catches it, and spins in the air with the athletic grace of an ice skater. He dribbles around a corner toward a moving trolley that's thirty feet ahead of him, chases it down, and leaps onto the back of the moving car. He hops off at the docks just in front of his family's restaurant and walks around to the back entrance. Hank opens the door, which rattles a little bell attached at the top of the doorframe. Carmela, Hank's nonna—the Italian word for grandmother—is a round woman in her late seventies, wearing a full apron and sitting at a table behind a shrimp pile. She looks up at Hank with a firm, cold stare as she performs the deveining process with an expert hand. His mother, Amalia, in her early forties and wrapped in an apron, smiles with a downward grin.

Carmela waggles her hand at Hank by joining her thumb to the rest of her fingers. "Siete in ritardo. Abbiamo mangiato già," (You are late. We ate already.) Hank kisses her and looks at a crab clock on the wall, reading 3:47 p.m. Carmela gets up, mumbling in Italian, washes her hands at the sink, dries them on her apron, and exits just as Stefano, dressed in a black suit and bow tie, enters.

Hank slips out of his shirt. "I'm sorry Pop, I—"

"You missed-a dinner. From now on, we going to church

11

together on-a Sunday, and then we come to work together."

Hank jerks his head forward and speaks with out-stretched arms, "But I work all day Saturday."

"We open Saturday and Sunday—and watch-a you tone of voice!"

Hank fires back, "When am I going to do my homework?"

"Don't worry about you homework. I'm-a you teach." Stefano smiles and puts his arm around his son, who lowers his head. "I take care of everything for you."

Hank looks into his father's large chestnut eyes. "But what if..."

Stefano folds his arms. "If-a what, Angelo?"

"I don't know... I—"

"Put on you suit. I need you next door." Stefano turns to walk out.

"Pop."

"Angelo, che cos'è?" (What is it?) Stefano asks in a short, agitated tone.

"When are you coming to one of my games?"

Stefano turns, shrugs his lips and shoulders, and walks out.

Hank looks at the little bell above the back door and then walks to the sink to wash. Amalia looks at her son with teary eyes and continues deveining. Hank snaps the water facet shut and rests his hands on the edges of the sink, his head hanging down and focusing on nothing. Water drips from his face into the sink as the sound of Amalia shelling shrimp and the ticking crab clock echoes in the room.

CHAPTER THREE

JOHN BUNN, A tall, silver-haired man in his early sixties, walks down a hallway at Stanford University located near Palo Alto California, roughly thirty miles from San Francisco. He's wearing a gray suit and carrying a black Trilby hat at his side. His eyes count the white doors along the corridor. After passing each door, his bright blue eyes discern the surroundings – up, left, and straight ahead. He pauses in front of a freshly shellacked oak door, strokes his chin with the backs of his fingers, extends his neck forward a bit to take a closer look, then touches the door with one finger to determine if it's dry. Just before he's about to knock, the door swings inward, and Dr. Richard Elliot, a natty dresser in his late fifties with male-pattern baldness and round, black-rimmed glasses, jets out. The two men nearly collide.

With a jovial smile, Dr. Elliot says, "Oh! You're a bit early, Mr. Bunn. I was just on my way to greet you at the main office."

John Bunn puts his hand flatly on his chest and bows his head slightly. "I apologize if I startled you, sir. I'm usually a bit ahead of schedule."

The two men laugh as people might in a formal setting, and Elliot welcomes Bunn inside with a wave of his hand. "Please come in."

"Thank you."

They walk into the spacious office until they reach a baroque oak desk. The office walls are adorned with an oak veneer and thick, ornate molding. Elliot settles into in a padded black leather chair, and Bunn sits across from him.

Elliot asks, "Can I get you something, water, tea?"

Mr. Bunn raises a large hand. "No thank you."

Elliot opens a folder on his desk and begins to read. Familiar with the document, he puts it down after a moment. "You were trained by the man who invented basketball, Dr. William Naismith, and you coached the University of Kansas to fifteen winning seasons." He pauses a moment. "Mr. Bunn, Stanford is among the top academic institutions in this nation, but we have a need to significantly upgrade our basketball program. Between 1923 and 1934 only Cal and Southern Cal have won Pacific Coast Conference titles, and I want Stanford's name added to that list."

Bunn nods.

Elliot opens the folder again, removes a document, and hands it to Bunn. "I made my decision so there's no need for formalities. I'd like to offer you the position as coach of the freshman team this season and to take over as the varsity coach next year."

Bunn glances at the paper and looks up at Elliot. "I'd be honored, sir."

Elliot extends his hand, "Welcome to Stanford University, Mr. Bunn."

They shake.

Elliot asks with squinted eyes, "What's the secret of your success?"

"No secret really. The game is fun and I love teachin' it. Some coaches forget about the fun part, but connectin' with kids on that level is the main difference 'tween a good team and a great one."

Elliot nods. "I see."

"I'm going to begin by visiting all the local high schools."

MADNESS

He waxes on about goals and plans.

Sitting upright with hands folded in a prayer-like pose on the desk, Elliot nods slowly, every now and again, in a relaxed, interested manner. His polished demeanor embodies years of honed professionalism, but hidden beneath the desk, his right leg pulses rapidly on the ball of his foot barely containing boyish excitement.

* * *

IN A BRIGHTLY lit office high rise, a middle-aged man with round tortoiseshell glasses, wearing a blue shirt speckled with tiny red diamonds, a matching bow tie, and red suspenders, sketches on a pad at night. His smoldering cigarette sits snugly in the groove of a black ashtray and sends a silky white ribbon slithering upward before thinning into the hazy air. He plucks it from the ashtray, raises it to his lips, and pulls in a long drag, brightening the glowing tip like a red firefly signaling for a mate. He gazes at his illustration of an apple tree and a spotted horse with a dead owl tied to it. He puts the cigarette back to his lips, picks up a pencil, and puts it to the paper. The dull pulse of automobiles on asphalt rises to the office. A ringing horn trumpets, and the sound of a screaming siren crescendos before it's slowly smothered by the vast network of skyscrapers, cars, and city streets.

* * *

HANK AND EDDIE have known each other most of their lives.

They become fast friends when Eddie convinces Hank to walk home from school with him the first week of first grade.

Once there, Hank has no idea how to get home. Eddie's mother, Gertrude or Trudy for short, takes Hank by the hand and walks him to the address he parrots to her. Amalia peers down the street with her hand in a salute position, blocking the sun from her eyes, when she sees Trudy holding Hank's hand on her right side and Eddie's on her left. The very day the boys become friends, so do their moms. Even though there is a stark difference between the two women—one being from Italy and the other an American native—they have much in common. Both are loving mothers with one child apiece, in a time when Italian and Irish families had five or more children due to the rhythm method, birth-control ordinance of the Roman Catholic Church.

The Kinsmans are transports from the Bronx, who moved to San Francisco a few years after the earthquake of 1906 when construction jobs were plentiful. Mrs. Kinsman is an overly polite individual who some refer to as dizzy. Regardless, she is a doting mother who makes sure Eddie eats all his meals and sleeps eight hours a night. She even warms the boy's underwear on the radiator before he goes to school on cool, damp San Francisco mornings. Eddie's father is silver haired, a few inches taller than Eddie, good humored, and quite the character. He's the kind of person who makes people laugh even though it's not his intention. Mr. Kinsman is a man's man who teaches Eddie about hunting, fishing, and guns, and made sure Eddie joined the Boy Scouts when he turned seven years old. Eddie often tried to get Hank to join, but between the family business, basketball, and school, Hank never had the time.

Whenever Hank isn't busy, he and Eddie are inseparable, and the tradition of walking to and from school continued from the first grade until graduation. Hank's basketball is now standard equipment after his gift from Ricky. It is on one of these journeys where Hank's nickname is born:

They have a leather belt strapped around their books, which are slung over their shoulders and dangle behind them as they walk.

Hank bounce passes to Eddie. "I wish I could change my name."

"Why?"

"I don't like it. It sounds too goody-goody."

"What would you change it to?"

"Anything but Angelo."

Eddie bounce passes back to Hank. "How about Hank? You look like my Uncle Henry. Everyone calls him Hank."

"Nah. Hank sounds like an old man."

Eddie snorts a laugh through his nose.

Hank laughs even though he doesn't know why they are laughing. "What's so funny?"

Eddie giggles deep in his throat and chokes out, "Hank Luisetti!" The giggle grows to a burst of laughter.

Hank shoots the ball at Eddie's head, but he catches it. "Nice try, Hank."

Hank, in an annoyed tone, says, "Okay, that's enough. It was funny but cut it out now."

Eddie stops laughing. "I'm not too fond of Fuzz, but sometimes things stick."

Hank chuckles. "I didn't start it on purpose. It just popped out."

Eddie looks at him with one raised brow. "I remember it well." Then he snaps his fingers. "Hey, you're not going to believe this, but remember that kid Joe DiMaggio who graduated from Galileo a few years ago?"

Hank thinks.

Eddie continues dribbling. "We played his team in baseball."

"Did you beat the hell out their catcher?"

"I was safe." He passes the ball to Hank. "I just heard that he plays for the Seals now."

Hank looks off into the distance. "I could only imagine a life like that. Besides playing a sport and getting paid for it, you get to travel from city to city. I bet they stay in the best hotels."

Eddie puffs up his chest. "That's one reason why I'm joining the Marines—to get away and to get that Marine bulldog tattooed right here." He makes a muscle pose with raised eyebrows.

Hank shoots a quick pass at Eddie's head, but he catches it again.

"Pretty good, Kinsman."

"Thank you." Eddie shoots back a pass.

Hank catches it. "That tattoo can get you killed, you know."

"At least my grandkids will know I died protecting their freedom overseas."

"Eddie?"

"Yeah?"

"You won't have grandkids."

"I will too." Eddie realizes his folly. "Oh yeah."

The boys laugh.

With a sly smirk and outstretched neck, Eddie says, "I guess I'll have to take care of that detail before I leave… heh, heh, heh!"

The basketball bounces off the side of Eddie's head with a thud, and his books fall to the ground. Eddie lunges for the rolling ball, but his mind moves faster than his legs, and he trips, falls on the ball, and rolls off. Hank, belly laughing, collapses to the ground, holding his stomach. He turns around to find Eddie running at him with the ball over his head, cocked and ready to launch. Eddie throws, but Hank catches it, and with the ball under his arm, grabs his books, leaps up, and dribbles away. Although Eddie runs full-out, a distance quickly grows between them. When Hank nears a crowded school yard, he is spotted by his friends.

Mac shouts, "Here comes Angelo!"

Mario calls with cupped hands, "I'm open, Ang!"

Mac, Mario, Yang, and Dabbs disperse into the crowd, each one calling for the ball. Hank hooks a sideways missile to Mario, and screams are heard as the ball whizzes just above the heads of a group of girls. A passing cycle zips on from the spirited boys, who pop out from the crowd like prairie dogs to catch sizzling passes. This is done partly for fun, but it's obvious that it's mostly done to get a reaction from the screaming girls, who are covering their heads and genuinely enjoying the game.

The school bell orders the teens to class, and they instinctively obey. As if under a spell, chaos melds into order while they herd themselves in the direction of the open arms of two large school doors.

* * *

A TALL GIRL with long, satiny, black hair tied up in a red ribbon—the same shade as her full, red lips—focuses her olive-shaped, suede-green cat eyes on the strikingly handsome boy bouncing a basketball and walking toward school with his shorter, sandy-haired friend. The boys have leather belts strapped around their books, which are slung over their shoulders and dangle behind them.

* * *

NED IRISH IS a thin, baby-faced man in his early thirties. Yet, his receding hairline, round, dark-rimmed glasses, and heavy Brooklyn accent make him seem older. He pulls his watch out by its chain, checks it, and then mechanically slips it back into the watch pocket of his vest. He studies the garish, theater-style marquee with the words Madison Square Garden spelled out in round light bulbs. Irish adjusts the grip on his brown leather briefcase and walks into the building. He walks out of an elevator and down a corridor to a doorway with a brass nameplate: General John Reed Kilpatrick - President. Irish sucks in a quick breath and knocks.

"Enter!" resonates as though coming from the belly of a bear.

Irish walks in.

General John Reed Kilpatrick, a full-lipped, thick eared, massive man in his sixties with short, white hair, is wearing a tailored suit accented with a gold collar post that pushes his tie knot into his windpipe. He's seated behind a large cherry-wood desk, absorbed in the sports section of the New York Times. Kilpatrick, without looking up, says, "State your business."

His voice cracks. "I'm Ned Irish—"

The general looks at him. "Speak up, son!"

Irish extends his hand—more as a peace offering than a polite greeting—and says in a mechanical, rehearsed manner, "I'm Ned Irish, sports writer for the World Telegram and publicity agent for the New York Giants."

"Do you have an appointment, son?"

Irish lowers his hand. "I do, sir."

Kilpatrick looks inquisitively at Irish while taking a cigar from a humidor. He drags the long cigar under his fleshy nose, inhaling with closed eyes, then he whispers, "Ah, Havana!"

As Irish talks, Kilpatrick slices off the cigar tip, snaps open a large chrome lighter, pushes the fat cigar into the flame, and takes a few short puffs.

Irish babbles, "I'm interested in promoting college basketball at the Garden... and with strong teams from LIU, St. John's, City College, and NYU, I can guarantee that college hoops will be the talk of the town with Madison Square Garden as its venue!"

Kilpatrick glares at him for a few seconds then laughs heartily from the diaphragm of his dense torso. Irish's smile is betrayed by his fair skin's inability to mask red.

When his fun is over, the general addresses Irish, "Using the Garden requires experience, significant finances, and a cast-iron backbone. Besides that, I hate listening to bullshit sales pitches... and I hate salesman. See yourself out."

Irish stares squarely at the big man before producing a folder from his briefcase. He places it on the desk and pushes it before Kilpatrick. "I'll guarantee the required four thousand dollars per event, and I'll control tickets, scheduling, and publicity. Also, the Garden will share in the profits above the guaranteed four grand on a percentage basis."

Kilpatrick glances at the folder and then looks suspiciously at Irish. "And how does a working man like you guarantee such significant finances?"

The two men lock eyes.

Perfectly timed, Irish reveals the hidden ace saved for this precise moment of the card game. "I have backing from Tim

Mara, owner of the New York Giants."

Kilpatrick squints at Irish from the corners of his puffy eyes while twirling a lit cigar between his lips.

CHAPTER FOUR

HANK WALKS OUT of the dean's office and is greeted by Eddie with a slap on the back.

"Hey, buddy. What was that about?"

They head to a row of lockers.

"He said if I want the privilege of bringing my basketball to school, I'll have to refrain from tossing it over people's heads in the schoolyard."

"Nothing gets past that guy."

Hank stops at a locker, unlocks it, and swings open the door with a bang. A group of teens look at Hank and laugh as they walk past. A wolf whistle is followed by a rise of laughter, which trails off down the hall. Five giggling cheerleaders in gold and black uniforms gather behind Hank. He turns around. Connie D'Angelo, the green-eyed, raven-haired beauty from the schoolyard, stands directly in front of Hank. She smiles with a tilted head.

Hank's Adam's apple bobs up and down with a gulp, but he recovers with, "Hi, Connie."

"Hello... Hank?"

With squinted eyes, he slowly turns his head in the direction of Eddie's toothy grin.

"Well..." Connie pauses for effect. "Is it true?"

"Did this numbskull put you up to this?" He jerks his thumb toward Eddie.

The girls snigger, and Eddie bolts away laughing.

Connie purses her puffy, red lips, reaches behind Hank, and pulls off a sign reading, "My name is Hank Luisetti, and

I wear girl's underwear."

Hank takes the paper, crumples it, and awkwardly laughs with his shoulders up around his ears. Eddie's guffawing bounces off the hallway walls.

"Excuse me."

The girls cackle as Hank takes off in the direction of Eddie's coughing laughter. Connie, biting her bottom lip, follows Hank with her eyes, then turns to her friends with a quick raise of her eyebrows.

A few hours later, a screaming school bell releases the kids from their holding cells. Hank, basketball under one arm, walks out of the room with Eddie. Both are wearing tank tops and shorts. After fighting their way through the river of teens pouring out of the building, they walk briskly down a hallway.

"We're even," says Hank. "I bopped you in the noggin with the basketball this morning, and you put that stupid sign on my back. I don't want to hear about Hank anymore. Deal?"

"Deal!"

They shake on it.

"Connie likes you, you know. You should ask her out."

"I don't go for girls like Connie."

Eddie chuckles.

"What's the matter?" Hank asks, scowling.

Eddie smiles, "You're scared of her!"

"I am not!"

"You are so full of crap, Hank. I mean, Angelo. Your knees start knocking when she's around, and you were so nervous this afternoon when she said 'Hi, Hank' that you broke wind."

"I did not—you idiot!"

MADNESS

"It was the silent kind, but I saw a curl of smoke come out of your shorts."

"Why would I be afraid of her?"

Eddie counts off using his fingers. "First of all, she's the prettiest girl in the school. Second, she's probably the prettiest girl in San Francisco. And third, her eyes alone could stop traffic on a Saturday afternoon."

Hank shakes his head. "That's not the reason."

"So, what's the reason? This, I have to hear."

"Remember Anna DeMone? One date and she had our kids' names picked out. Besides, I want someone who didn't grow up in the neighborhood."

"I wouldn't mind Connie picking out my kids' names."

A closed-lip smile slowly spreads across Hank's face.

They walk into the gymnasium. Yang, Dabbs, Mac, and Mario, the resident juniors, and a group of underclassmen are gathered together.

Dabbs shouts, "Hey, it's Hank and Fuzzy!"

Everyone laughs.

Hank looks at Eddie. "You're dead!"

Eddie sprints away with Hank in pursuit.

Mac cups his hands to his mouth. "It does have a ring to it... Hank Luisetti."

More laughter erupts from the crew.

Hank, now among them, says, "I don't care how it rings." He grabs Eddie and playfully tackles him to the ground. Hank's basketball rolls away.

A piercing whistle snaps everyone's head to Ricky Durán, jogging toward them with a bloated canvas bag over his shoulder and a black whistle clenched between his teeth. "Alright boys we've got a lot to do today." He looks at Hank. "Oh hello, Hank!"

Amid more laughter, Hank shakes his head.

"The Amador Valley Dons lost last night, so for the first time in nine years—" Cheers and roughhousing erupt, but Ricky raises his voice to compensate, "—the Galileo Lions will be playing in the semifinals!"

The celebratory cheers continue, but a few quick blasts of Ricky's whistle bring order.

"Everybody take a knee."

The team kneels.

Ricky makes eye contact with each player as he sweeps around the semicircle. "Making it to the semis is good, but is it enough?"

The boys remain focused on their coach.

"For me, enough is nothing short of the state championship trophy sitting in a display case in these halls."

Some of them nod and others remain fixed.

"As you know, Galileo has won the states in swimming, baseball, and football, but never in basketball, so this is a special opportunity. If we win the next four, we get the honor to play for that trophy at the University of San Francisco gymnasium."

A few kids clap.

"We have the worst record of all the teams in the semis, but we will use that to our advantage because no one expects us to win."

Mac asks, "Who are we playing first?"

"I'll find out tomorrow, but I'm not done... I took a trip to a Mississippi Valley tournament this weekend so I could see what's happening beyond our league. I really wanted to travel to New York to see the teams that set the standard for the rest of us, but it was a little beyond my reach this year. However, Mississippi Valley introduced me to a new style of play, and it got me thinking." He pauses. "If we can implement a few of these changes, we could rattle our competition."

"What was it like?" Hank asks.

"They weren't stuck to the man-to-man mindset; they followed the ball instead of the man. Another amazing thing is that every now and then they shot with one hand. I'm not asking you to learn the one-handed shot, but—"

"One hand?" asks Yang with a smirk.

Intrigued, Hank asks, "Can you show me?"

"I'd like to focus on their philosophy, because we can't master a new shot in a week, but I'll give you an idea of the mechanics behind it." Reaching into his canvas bag for a ball, he talks more to himself. "It was really quite fascinating."

The team stands, some rub their knees, but all eyes are on Ricky. He holds the ball in his right hand and steadies it underneath with the fingertips of his left hand. Yang and Ron look at each other and then back at Ricky. Hank uses his own ball to mirror Ricky's movements.

Ricky hesitates before shooting. "I'm not sure if this is exactly right, but here goes."

He shoots and misses. Yang and Ron stifle laughter.

Hank faces the basket, steadies his form, and shoots. The ball resembles a missile homing in on its target as it arcs through the air and sweeps through the net. Openmouthed, he jerks his neck at Ricky while pointing at the basket. His friends cheer the shot. Ricky dips into his canvas bag, grabs a ball, and tosses it to Hank who crouches low and bounces it forcefully and deliberately a few times. Finally, he rises to his shooting position, and the ball flows into place like a spinning yo-yo gliding back to its owner's hand. With a silky flick of his wrist, Hank gets the ball to leap away, locate the rim, and dive through the net with a raspy swish.

His teammates scramble for a loose ball. Dabbs shoots a one-handed brick, but Ricky's whistle interrupts the chaos.

"Begin with drill one, but I want the ball shot with one hand. Let Hank shoot first so you can watch his form. Let's see if we can use this shot next week."

The coach's eyes are fixed on Hank as he sets up his teammates in two vertical lines beginning at the half-court line. Ricky blows his whistle to begin the drill, and the team sprints into action. He blows it again two hours later, and the dampened, red-faced team drag themselves over and gather around.

"Are we going to win next week?!"

"Yes!" the team says in unison.

"I can't hear you!"

"Yes!" they shout.

"Still can't hear you!"

"Yes!" they scream.

"That's the way I want to hear it! See you tomorrow."

The team breaks toward the exit, and Hank jogs to his basketball on the sideline.

Ricky walks by and puts his hand on Hank's shoulder. "Practice that one-hander. I think you two were made for each other."

Hank wipes the sweat off his brow with the back of his forearm. "I'll be practicing at the park tonight."

Eddie's voice rings out in the exit stairwell with a lingering, "So long, Hank!"

Hank's head shoots up. "Oh, that's it!" He scoops up the ball and charges the doorway.

* * *

MADNESS

AT SEVEN O'CLOCK that evening, Hank is alone in the park as he threads his way around the familiar pattern of cracks and potholes. At the foul line, he leaps and releases a one-hander. The ball flies from his fingertips, slams into the backboard, and ricochets through the net.

Ricky Durán walks his German Shepard through a snipped opening in the fence just below the No Trespassing sign. He shakes his head and smiles as he walks to Hank, his dog barking at the teen.

Hank turns toward the sound, then raises his hand like a student who's excited to answer a question. "Mr. Durán!" He sprints to his coach as the dog drags Ricky to the overzealous boy. "Mr. Durán! You're not going to believe it!" He bends down and rustles the dog's head. "Hey, Lady!"

Lady runs in circles, and Ricky points to his watch. "I've only got a minute, my wife—"

"The one-handed shot changes everything! It's not so much about shooting as it is about movement! Two hands disrupt your rhythm. Stopping to shoot or pass gives a defender reaction time, but with one hand you're free!"

Ricky glances at his watch. "They only used it occasionally over there… Angelo, I—"

"Then they missed the point!"

"Not here! Bad dog!" Ricky pulls his urinating dog off the court. "Ang—"

"This shot frees your mind. You aren't thinking about stopping. Let me show you something. I'm going to drive toward the basket. Cross behind me near the foul line." Hank runs a few steps to retrieve the ball. "You've got to see this, Mr. Durán!"

Ricky looks at his watch, ties Lady to the pole, and positions himself as Hank drives toward the basket. The coach crosses behind Hank as instructed, then the boy bounce passes behind himself to Ricky who receives the pass and shoots. Ricky smiles and nods his head a few times just before Lady grabs the ball.

With outstretched arms, Hank asks, "Great, huh?" He gets the ball from Lady. "You see, I'm not thinking of stopping. It's one motion. Now, in this next play, try to stop me." He jogs to half court and asks Ricky to start at the foul line. Hank begins his movement forward and the two drive toward each other. When they meet, he bounces the ball behind his back, leaps, and Ricky jumps up to block. Hank leans back in a forty-five-degree angle and shoots. The ball sails over Ricky's hands and gets swallowed by the net.

"Wow! That was incredible, Angelo. Incredible!"

Lady runs for the ball but is snapped back when her chain runs out.

"I can fake out defenders and feed the open man. I won't hog the ball, Coach. I want to feed the man closest to the net."

"But shoot when you can, Angelo! You don't have to always look to pass even if someone is closer than you. You're a superior shooter, and this new shot will make you deadly."

Hank blinks twice and asks without direct eye contact, "You want to play some one-on-one?"

"That was a compliment, Angelo. Being polite and humble is great but learning how to acknowledge a compliment is important too. It's not being conceited to do that."

Hank smiles awkwardly. "Okay. Hey, do you want to play?"

Ricky looks at the boy. "Sure, we still have a good ten minutes of sunlight."

Hank holds up his finger in a wait position before jogging over to the ball, which is just out of Lady's reach. She whimpers as Hank turns away.

He points to the sad-eyed pooch lying down with her head resting on her paws. "Can she rebound for us?"

Ricky nods.

In the fading sunlight, two silhouettes engage in joyful competition on the broken playground court while a barking dog serves as the howling fans of a jam-packed arena.

CHAPTER FIVE

ALTHOUGH RICKY DURÁN coaches his team to the semi-finals, it is Luisetti who leads the Lions to victory over the next four games. Hank uses the freedom of the running one-handed shot to rewrite the game's traditional mindset. Ricky's permission to roam the court has Hank everywhere; he brings up the ball, rebounds, and creates situations that leave his teammates wide open near the basket.

In a game against the Lowell Cardinals, Hank receives a pass from Eddie and is smothered by a defender waving his outstretched arms like a spinning windmill. Hank fakes a move right and cuts left, leaving the windmill behind. Mac's defender sees Hank alone and breaks away to cover him. Hank pivots left, bounce passes to Mac on the right, and continues motoring toward the basket. The windmill and Mac's defender follow Hank for a few steps before they realize that he doesn't have the ball. Unguarded, Mac comfortably lofts a two-handed shot through the net. The whistle calls the boys to the center circle for a jump ball. The windmill looks at his teammate and shakes his head.

In the next leg of the tournament against the Archbishop Riordan Crusaders, Dabbs passes to Hank on the left, and he dribbles across the court. Hank passes to Eddie, who crosses him at the foul line. Eddie takes a shot, but the ball is deflected sky high by a defender. All eyes watch the ball as if it were stacks of dollar bills dropping from the ceiling. The greedy teens bunch up and leap, but Hank, the greediest, leaps above them, snags the prize, and passes the ball backward over his head to Yang while he is still high in the air. Yang receives the pass and dribbles in for an easy layup. The opposing coach, a pot-bellied man wearing a gold V-neck sweater and brown tie, says to himself, "What in the hell just happened?"

* * *

WHEN COACHES DECIDE to double-team Hank, it leaves his teammates open, which is what Hank prefers. If they leave Hank open, however, they feel the effects of that unstoppable one-handed shot, so coaches mostly double up on him. While Hank only averages five points a game, he is responsible for nearly every other point scored due to his masterful all-around play. When he swishes a one-hander, the fans gasp, then cheer in amazement—even those from the opposing team.

* * *

IN THE FINAL game of the semifinals, the Lions are over-matched by the team favored to win the states. The Palo Alto Vikings are taller, more agile, more experienced, and more athletic than the Lions. The Lions have Hank, who manages to keep them ahead for most of the game, but it's a dogfight. He has a much harder time getting the ball to his teammates and becomes overheated by relentless pressure. When Ricky rests Hank, the Vikings move ahead, so he sees no other option than to keep him in.

Hank is nearly out of gas by the start of the fourth quarter, and the Vikings have the chance they've been waiting for. Their plan to wear Hank down has paid off. They gain steam in the latter half of the fourth quarter, tying the game at thirty-two with two minutes left. The momentum is on the side of the Vikings, whose home crowd resembles an iron-age Scandinavian hoard adorned in horned helmets, plastic swords and battle axes. Ricky calls a time out to stop the bleeding and reengage his team. The sweaty, trodden Lions form a half circle around their coach, who is as sweaty as they are.

Ricky bites off his words and spits them out as he speaks, "Did you guys give up? They've just tied us with three unanswered goals! We lose tonight, and it's over. We win, and we play in the championship. Our season comes down to two minutes! Are you going to be talked about at Galileo for years after you graduate?"

Some boys nod, others wipe sweat away. They all pant.

"Eddie, I want you more aggressive in the zone."

Eddie nods. "Okay. Nobody gets past me."

Ricky looks to Yang. "You grab every single rebound — no exceptions. Every rebound is yours!"

Yang nods.

"Angelo, you're defending number twelve too closely. He's nothing but a floorwalker."

Hank looks confused.

"He's not a shooter, so back off him. Most importantly, what we need from you is points. I need you to pour it on!"

Hank stares up at his coach.

Ricky looks at Hank but only sees the ten-year-old boy practicing at the lopsided park, so he softens his tone. "We need you, Angelo!"

Hank scans the faces of his teammates for approval, then looks at Ricky. "Okay, Mr. Durán."

Ricky claps twice, the team claps twice, and they break and jog on the court. Yang and a tall Viking get into position for a center jump. The referee releases the ball, and the Viking tips it to Floorwalker. Hank backs off, then he juts in, steals it, and weaves around defenders before they have time to react. When he approaches the top of the key, he swishes one through the hoop. Ricky punches the air, and for the next two minutes, Hank schools the Vikings with three straight baskets—swish, after swish, after swish. One shot is an astonishing forty-footer. The buzzer sounds, and Hank gets mauled by his exuberant teammates.

The young star is carried around on the shoulders of his team, past the Galileo cheerleaders. Connie winks at him when he passes her, and the two lock eyes as he is paraded away.

Watching the game from the first row of the balcony, John Bunn takes a pen and pad from his jacket pocket. The paper contains several handwritten names—some are circled, others crossed out. He makes a star next to Luisetti, puts the card in his pocket, taps it twice, and joins the crowd flowing toward the exit.

* * *

MOUNTING PRESSURE GROWS in the week leading up to the state championship. Ricky continues the daily practices, which serve more as a stress reliever than anything else. Although the team earned its spot, the magnitude of their success begins to sink in after the Viking upset, and the championship game at the University of San Francisco is unfamiliar ground. Besides the fact that it is their first state championship, they have never played in front of thousands of people before. The USF budget provides an impressive arena with a large scoreboard, plate glass backboards, rows and rows of bleachers, and a new floor that glistens like the top of a frozen pond after a spring rain.

The spectators are a combination of college students, locals, and fans from both the Lions and their opponents, the Los Gatos Wildcats. The Wildcats have played in several state championships and are the winners of five. For them, this is the expected destination. Both teams have plenty of room for cheerleaders, who jump up for quick cheers after a rebound or score.

Connie, decked out in sparkly gold and black, sits center and leads her cheer squad. The Lions wear gold tank tops with the word Galileo arced in a half circle above their number—both the name and number are black. The backs have a picture of a lion head under the number. The shorts, which are nearly the equivalent of a satiny Speedo, are gold with two thin, black, horizontal stripes running up the sides, piped in black around the edges. They wear black, high-top sneakers, and most players wear black knee pads. Hank, number seventeen, feels as though pads slow his game, so he forgoes the extra equipment. The Wildcats are dressed in nearly identical uniforms. The only differences are their colors, black with orange lettering, and Los Gatos is written in a semicircle over their number on the front of their shirts.

From the first jump through the end of the fourth quarter, Galileo is on the lower side of the score. Similar to the Vikings, the taller, more accomplished Wildcats focus squarely on Hank. If they can stop his passing game, they will add a sixth championship trophy to their showcase. The Wildcat coach tells his boys to leave number seventeen some room to pass. They bate Hank in an effort to snatch the ball from his dependent teammates.

With ninety seconds remaining, the Wildcats are on top

by a score of 31 to 32, but another basket brings it to 31 to 34, with one minute on the clock. Ricky Durán calls a timeout in hopes of replicating the heroics from a week ago.

John Bunn looks on from the stands.

Hank, Eddie, Dabbs, Mac, and Yang gather around Ricky who, once again, is as disheveled as his team. Like a sergeant sending his boys into hostile terrain, Ricky rallies his troops with hope and fury.

"We were here before and came away victorious! You earned this spot, and you will not allow them to take it from you! You worked too hard, and we are too close to victory! That championship trophy will be ours in just a few minutes if you do exactly as I tell you." He drags a towel across his face to mop cascading sweat. "We can eke out two plays and win this, but get the ball to Angelo." He turns to his star player and says, "We need four points, Angelo! Four points and it's ours."

This time, Hank does not seek approval from his teammates. Instead, he nods and repeats the command, "Four points!"

The whistle orders them back on court. Ricky claps twice, the team claps twice, and they rush into their positions for the center jump. Yang and his Wildcat counterpart face each other in the center of the circle. On the circle's outer rim are two men on either side of the centers—two to the right and two to the left. The other four are scattered about. This inner circle around the ball is the hottest spot on the court. Sweat droplets drizzle to the floor from their faces and hair, and a pungent stench of B.O. hovers.

As the ref positions the ball between Yang and the Wildcat center, muscles twitch on the boys in the hot circle, who push against each other, preparing for the tap. Hank, to

Yang's right, screws his eyes onto the ball. The ref releases the ball between them. The Wildcat center swats it, but Hank snarls and rips it out of the air. He drives it toward the basket and is met head on by a tall, lanky Wildcat who plants his spindly legs and waves his long arms. Hank sees Dabbs alone in the right forward position calling for the ball. He fakes right to Dabbs, but spins left, shoots, and sinks a thirty-foot, one-handed bank shot.

The repercussion of the shot detonates the arena. Fans stand and cheer, animated coaches bark orders from the side-lines, and cheerleaders' mouths move, but their rallying cries are muted by the screaming stadium. Hank feels the cheers as vibrations, bouncing off his chest and buzzing through him from the gym floor.

As they head to half-court, Dabbs comes up behind Hank and speaks in his ear, "They are going to be all over you. If it gets too hot, feed me in the corner. I was wide open a minute ago."

Dabbs slaps Hank's butt and moves into position. The teams gather around for the center jump with ten seconds left on the clock. Yang taps it between Hank and his defender. Both touch it simultaneously, but Hank rips it away and motors toward the basket. He is met by two defenders in the same location as the previous basket. Hank has a shot before they approach him, but he hesitates when he sees Dabbs waving his arms.

Ricky panics.

Hank jumps up and sends a bullet to Dabbs who is all alone. Dabbs sets, shoots, and misses. The horn sounds.

Hank stands frozen on the glistening court floor among celebrating Wildcats. A sea of black and orange streams past him.

MADNESS

Ricky shuts his eyes and clenches his jaw from the gut-punching finale.

Connie gazes at Hank who looks injured by the jubilant faces, passionate hugs, and celebratory noise of the new state champions.

Guilt forces him to watch.

He remains fixed in place, staring, unable to tear his eyes from his gaffe. Eddie walks over, puts his arm around his friend, and leads him to Ricky who is seated with the rest of the team on the sideline.

John Bunn, biting his bottom lip, takes it all in from the stands above.

CHAPTER SIX

TWO WEEKS PASS after the basketball season imploded at the USF arena, and Hank's life returns to schoolwork, park basketball, and Angelo's Frutti Di Mare Ristorante. But the air surrounding the restaurant becomes noxious as Angelo's becomes Stefano's obsession.

The lifelong dream he cultivated for his only son is on the verge of reality, and he can barely contain his euphoria. Stefano wastes no opportunity to educate Hank on finances, inventory, menu options, daily specials, employees, and above all, a costly remodeling project and grand reopening of both the fish store and Angelo's. Stefano scrimped and saved for ten years to make this renovation a surprise graduation gift for Hank. Discussions with contractors are underway and work will begin in September. When Stefano isn't preaching to Hank, he fantasizes about his plans. At times the father breaks away from his fantasies and looks at his son with beaming admiration; he just smiles and nods his head. Hank smiles back, a smile that brews lava in his stomach and sends hot swirls of anxiety churning in his gut.

Hank's charade dupes Stefano, but Amalia knows them both and fears the mounting tumult, realizing they are unaware that a tiny spark of truth will ignite a familial bomb. Amalia diverts their attention when she senses a possible crisis by serving food, dropping a glass or dish, or planning emergencies such as forgetting something at the restaurant. Hank's graduation is a few months away. Perhaps by June, her son's apprehension will burn away like fog in the powerful

MADNESS

San Francisco sun.

* * *

MONDAYS ARE ALWAYS the best day of the week for the Luisettis. Even though the fish store is open, the restaurant is closed, and the Luisettis spend family time together. When Hank was a child, they would have picnics, take long drives, or rent a boat to go fishing or cruise the bay. As Hank reached his teens, Mondays took on a new meaning because it was a day away from his family, a time for hanging out with friends and getting in as much basketball as possible.

On one such Monday afternoon, after a few hours of hoops, Hank and Eddie enter Hank's kitchen from the back entrance of the house. As the bridge between the back entrance and the rest of the home, the Luisetti kitchen is a relatively small but busy room. The four-compartment oak icebox is fairly new and has shiny brass hardware. Hank puts his basketball on a kitchen chair and takes an apple from a basket on top of the icebox while Eddie sits at the table.

Hank tosses an apple to Eddie and says, "I still can't believe we lost." He grabs a knife from a drawer and begins peeling the skin off the apple into a container on the counter.

"We had Huey and Calbi's little brother. Of course we lost." Eddie takes a monster bite, and juice drips down his chin, which he wipes away with his hand.

Hank shakes his head. "I'm talking about the states, knucklehead."

"Oh... Why are you still thinking about it? We did great. We only lost by one basket."

"That's why I'm still thinking about it."

Eddie takes a few quick chunks out of the apple and looks at a stack of mail on the table. He picks up the top envelope and reads, "Master Angelo Luisetti. Hey, you got a letter from Stanford University."

Hank tilts his head before tossing the apple on the counter, grabbing the letter, and opening it.

"What do you think they want?' Eddie asks.

Hank's finger zig zags across the page. His lips are moving but he only utters an occasional "S." Finally, he reads aloud, "...awarding you a full athletic scholarship..." Hank smacks his forehead, then grips his hair. "Holy crap! Holy crap! Holy crap, Eddie! Stanford University wants me to enroll in their school and play basketball for them!"

Eddie grabs Hank, picks him up, and they wrestle around the room.

"What the hell-a you doing? You gonna break-a the kitch!" Hank's grandmother says, entering the room.

"Nonna, I'm going to college!"

"Che cosa?" ("What?")

Eddie runs over to Carmela and hugs her off the ground.

"What the hell-a you craze!"

The boys explode into laughter, and Eddie puts her down.

Carmela opens a drawer, takes out a wooden spoon with a burnt handle, and shakes it at Eddie. "You not-a too old for this."

Eddie and Hank laugh harder. Eddie releases a high-pitched, part-laugh, part-scream and grabs Hank again. Carmela runs after Eddie and smacks him on the butt with the spoon. He breaks away and runs around rubbing his butt.

Thunder cracks and the sound of fat raindrops smack the window just as Stefano and Amalia, wearing jackets and carrying groceries, enters the kitchen.

"We just made it!" Stefano says.

Hank's smile fades.

Silence.

Eddie grabs a grocery bag from Amalia and puts it on the table.

One look at Hank and Amalia senses trouble, so she blurts out, "Eddie, you stay for dinner, tonight. Yes?"

Eddie responds politely. "I'd love to Mrs. Luisetti, but I can't." He looks at Hank and says with a quick shake of the head, "See you later, buddy."

When Eddie looks at Carmela, she makes a sideways chopping motion at him. He winks at her and walks out. Amalia glances down at the table and sees Eddie's apple and the letter. Stefano notices her glance, puts down his bag, and picks up the document.

As Stefano reads, Hank rubs his hands on his thighs.

Smiling weakly, he says, "I'm going to college, Pop… Isn't that great?"

Stefano flips over the letter and smiles. "What-a you think I'm-a stupe." He joins his fingers in an upturned point and waggles his hand. "You play too much. Help-a you mama with-a the food, Angelo." Stefano takes off his coat.

Hank doesn't move.

Carmela leaves the room. Amalia takes items from the grocery bag and carries a large jar of red peppers to the counter. It "slips" out of her hands and shatters on the floor. Hank and Stefano do not flinch as the smell of vinegar fills the room.

"Everybody calls me Hank, Pop."

Stefano glares. His eye twitches once, and Amalia wrings her hands.

"I'm going to college."

Spoken through his teeth, Stefano says, "You goin' nowhere!"

"Only if I stay here."

Stefano becomes ugly with anger, then calms. He walks over and puts his hand on Hank's shoulder. "You don't need-a no school. I'm-a you teach. Remember?"

"This is about basketball. It's what I want. If you watched me play, you'd understand."

Stefano raises his voice. "Who's-a poison you mind? Ricky Durán?" He storms toward the back door.

Hank swipes the letter and cuts off his father.

Amalia gasps.

Hank holds the letter in front of Stefano. "Mr. Durán doesn't even know about this yet, and it has nothing to do with him or you. It has to do with me! This is an honor, Pop."

Stefano snags the letter, rips it in half, and flings the pieces into the air.

As the pieces flit to the ground around Hank, he closes his eyes for a beat, opens them, and looks directly at Stefano with contempt. "I'm still going, Pop. The restaurant was your idea. It's what you wanted. You never asked me what I wanted." Sharpened words fly from Hank's mouth like knives. "I'm not ever taking over the restaurant! I never wanted it! This is my life—mine—and nobody will ever force a future on me again!"

Stefano slaps Hank across the face, but he doesn't flinch.

Amalia shrieks, "Stefano!"

Her husband's countenance changes as he is struck by a thought. He's won this battle. He looks at his son and says with his hands on his hips, "How are you gonna pay for school? I'm not-a give you one penny!"

Straight-faced, emotionless, Hank confidently delivers

the blow. "They think I'm so good, they are paying for me to go."

Stefano fires back with both barrels. "This is the way you treat me after all I do for you! You my son no more!"

Hank's shell cracks and tears well in his eyes. He picks up the pieces of the letter from the floor, grabs his jacket, and bolts out of the house.

Amalia looks at Stefano with her hands over her mouth and runs out of the room.

Stefano gathers the shards of glass from the broken jar and cuts his finger. He walks to the sink, runs water over his sliced skin and stares at the blood streaming down the drain.

Several hours later, Hank sits alone in a thunderstorm on a bench at the Spring Valley Playground basketball courts. Ropes of sideways rain strike at him relentlessly. He hunches his shoulders forward, raises his collar, and fists the jacket under his neck while peering vacantly into the black night as waves of windy rain sweep across the cracked asphalt.

CHAPTER SEVEN

AFTER TRUTH MADE its first appearance at the Luisetti's, Hank is strictly forbidden to step foot in the fish store or restaurant again. Stefano cancels the renovations and grand reopening gala.

Time passes, however, and the suffocation associated with living his father's dream ends. Hank's feelings about the restaurant change—he half-misses the place. He enjoys the rush of customers who form a line along the bar and out the door between seven and nine every weekend night.

Hank is a favorite among the customers due in part to his entertaining athleticism. He can balance more plates of food on his arm than a circus performer, and he cleans and sets tables with such speed that one day, a customer quipped, "Jesus, I can't even think that fast."

Hank also enjoys the regulars. Arthur is a placid, friendly, white-haired widower in his eighties who sits at the bar every night and orders a dozen clams on the half shell, an Italian entrée, and Dewar's on the rocks. The Murphy's, Shamus and Maureen, love anything topped with tomato sauce and gooey parmesan cheese and come to Angelo's every Saturday night. They arrive just before the seven o'clock rush and sit at table fifteen under the bay window. They have practiced this ritual nearly every week since the restaurant opened and always ask Hank to tell them his basketball stories.

Besides the restaurant, Hank misses Stefano's admiration as he has always been the light of his father's life. Stefano taught Hank to fish, ride a bicycle, and cook, as well as the basics of plumbing, carpentry, and electricity. When Hank was a child, Stefano told him stories, prayed with him every night, and worked with him every day until he perfected his times tables. Now, Stefano walks out of a room if Hank walks into it, and the former fond looks turn to ones of repugnance and disappointment. This sudden turn of events weighs on Hank, so he learns to distract himself by playing lots of basketball, spending more time with his friends, and reading — which he figures will better prepare him for college life.

* * *

ONE NIGHT, WHILE Hank is in his room poring over a Stanford catalog, he hears his parents arguing. It is rare for them to argue, mostly because of Amalia's patience. Both Jesus and her parents taught her that husbands were the head of the household. Since quarreling is rare, it always makes Hank uneasy. He either paces in his room or reads away the knot in the pit of his stomach until the bout is over. This particular row is especially punishing for Hank because he is the cause. They shed their English shackles and let it fly in soul-quenching Italian rhythms. Hank is fluent in Italian, so he understands every word, and since Italian is his foreign tongue, hearing it used in the argument makes it all the more dramatic.

The drama, however, is a farce. Stefano instigates this perfectly staged fight with his wife, using Amalia as collateral damage. The argument is not between husband and wife but between father and son — the time-honored tradition of parental manipulation.

Like an actor who has carefully primed his audience for the big moment, Stefano switches to English for his dramatic climax. "I'm selling the restaurant to Dante!"

Amalia breaks into tears. Stefano exits the stage with the slam of a door, and guilt's sharp edge finds its target listening from the upstairs bedroom. The foundation of Hank's dreams snaps under the weight of family expectation and deception.

After a few hours, Hank decides to tell his parents that he will decline Stanford's offer and take over the restaurant as originally planned. He swears to himself and makes a deal with God. He looks up to the heavens and says he is sorry for being so ungrateful, pledges that he will not disrespect his parents again, and writes down what he will say in his apology, so he won't forget anything.

But like most promises made in the heat of passion or in the midst of naiveté, Hank feels differently in a few days. Whenever he plans to recite his speech, some excuse surfaces. He can always do it the next day.

In the meantime, Hank remembers snatches of Principal Barker's graduation address. Barker spoke about how many view graduation as an end, but commencement actually means beginning—the beginning of life's long journey. He talked in metaphors about how this was the most exciting time of life. The future, he said, is "a vast, unknown wilderness." He also spoke of the future as a white canvas, and that "high school has provided you with the paint to create your own personal masterpiece." Principal Barker had a knack for making everything he said sound important—even the morning announcements that always ended with, "and everybody be good today." He concluded his speech by saying, "The very moment you leave this building you are stepping out onto a bridge and only you get to decide where that bridge will lead." It drew thunderous applause.

Barker's speech also reaffirms Hank's notions that his father's paint-by-number canvas of the restaurant—a house on Russian Hill, a wife, kids, grandkids, and death, is not what he wants. Reemerging thoughts of Stefano's version of Hank's future wrap around his windpipe like a snake. He is standing directly in the middle of Barker's Bridge, because while Hank hasn't told his father about his plans to take over Angelo's, he also has ignored Stanford's admission deadlines.

It isn't until John Bunn calls Hank one evening and tells him that he only has one day to commit, that Hank makes his decision. He calls Ricky Durán and asks if he will drive him to Stanford the following day. With that settled, he walks over to Eddie's house to wish him well—the night before the two lifelong friends' futures will lead them in opposing directions.

* * *

THE WALLS OF the Kinsman residence are decorated with mounted fish, deer heads, framed sailboat paintings, and religious articles. Eddie's father sits in an armchair in their screened-in porch, uncommon in Russian Hill, reading a magazine. Hank rings the doorbell, and Big Ed doesn't move even though he sits ten feet from the door. Gertrude rushes in while removing her housecoat.

She is startled when she sees Ed senior sitting on the porch, "Oh! You're still here?"

Without looking up, he says, "No, I'm over there... What do you mean I'm still here?"

"I thought you went to the Gilbert's to borrow his card table."

Hank rings the bell again.

"The squirrels are looking for you."

Trudy laughs and slaps the air. "Stop, Eddie. I thought

you left."

She opens the door and smiles at Hank who's wearing a faded Galileo T-shirt.

"Hello, Mrs. Kinsman."

"Oh hello, Angelo. You've come to say goodbye? How sweet of you. It seems like you two were playing with your toy soldiers just yesterday."

"Hello, Mr. Kinsman."

"Hey, how's it going there?" Big Ed rises to greet Hank. While shaking his hand, Ed looks into Hank's eyes with a stiff upper lip as he squints. "Good handshake, son. You can always tell what kind of a man someone is by his handshake. Your friend's upstairs packing for the Marines. Tomorrow at 0500 hours, he'll be on his way to Camp Pendleton."

He smiles and makes his way up the stairs.

When Hank enters the room, Eddie is seated on his bed feeding an open knapsack.

"Your father's in rare form tonight. He just gave me the handshake."

They mimic the stiff-lipped, squinty-eyed handshake pose as they speak.

Eddie imitates his father's voice. "We're doing this as a test of strength and honor. As men!"

Hank takes over as Big Ed. "Yes, men! We're shaking and staring each other down, feeling for weakness."

Eddie laughs and Hank smiles, but his expression abruptly changes. Eddie goes back to packing. After a beat, he asks, "He still hasn't spoken to you?"

Pacing the room, Hank says, "I almost backed out of it. Stanford's orientation was yesterday. My father did everything for me. He sacrificed, planned, and saved all his money for me, and I let him down. I broke his heart, but I can't stay in Russian Hill my whole life! I always knew it, but I couldn't tell him. I thought I could live the life he planned for me." He stops pacing, leans his elbow on a dresser, and rubs his forehead.

Eddie stops packing and looks at his friend. "You weren't born to work in a fish store or a restaurant. I knew you weren't going to do it. You were born to play basketball, and your father will understand that one day. Trust me, Hank, it'll all work itself out. You're doing the right thing."

Hank looks at his friend and nods his head slowly. "I don't have a brother, Eddie... You're it."

"You're it too... Friends since first grade."

Hank thinks of that first day when Eddie and Gertrude walked him home. "Friends since we were five." His eyes jerk open. "I've got to get going. I haven't even started packing. Mr. Durán is driving me to Stanford tomorrow morning."

He turns his open palm toward Eddie. The two thrust their hands to each other, which smack together with a clap. They squeeze each other's hands with one powerful shake and hold it there, tight-mouthed. This is not a test of strength among men as they had previously mocked. They are two men using it to suffocate the vulnerability they're feeling at the moment, realizing they will be leaving each other after spending an entire childhood together.

Eddie speaks first. "Knock 'em dead out there, Angelo."

"Take care of yourself, Private."

A smiling Hank salutes his friend, and he walks out of the room.

CHAPTER EIGHT

PEOPLE SPEND A lot of time fabricating the exact details of their futures. Perfectly choreographed scenes run though the mind like a film, and the writer is also the director, casting director, producer, star, and audience. The author is so skillful, he or she can also perform the starring role in any imagined scene, and the all-consuming highlight reel plays itself over and over again. This fiction is so powerful that it touches people in real time, as the visions can either cripple them or create a heightened sense of euphoria. It will even play at night as daydreams segue to night dreams—or nightmares. The scenes continue until the conflict is resolved or the repetition of the action dulls the senses. It works the same with the past, as people either exaggerate the positive or beat themselves up over negative events that cannot be undone; yet, they write a new script fictionalizing nonfiction, and making it play out according to perceptions, whims, and expectations. These visions can be many things, but they can never be the truth. They are built upon the author's fantasies, a mere figment of his or her imagination. Such is the case with Hank when he imagines what will happen if he leaves Russian Hill.

There was a time when he imagined stealing his father's truck and driving as fast and as far as he could with no predetermined destination. He'd just clobber the gas peddle, leaving a trail of smoke and debris as pieces of the truck blew off, while his father's figure shrunk in the rear-view mirror. Sometimes, he'd imagine living in the truck and waitering his way through every major city in the country. He'd visit the

MADNESS

Grand Cannon, Niagara Falls, the White House, the Mississippi River, the Great Lakes, the Statue of Liberty, and the Empire State Building. Of course, he'd find parks along the way and shoot hoops with anyone willing to play. Those were the light, action-adventure-type dreams.

Since the Stanford scholarship and subsequent Stefano War, however, Hank now writes a different scene. In this version, he is in the kitchen with his suitcases, but his father stages one last attempt to keep him from leaving. Stefano slams his fist on the table as he threatens, harasses, and screams while Amalia's sobs slice Hank's flesh to ribbons.

As the days draw closer, the scenes become more intense. On his final night at home, Hank tosses and turns the night away. While his restlessness mimics the last night of vacation before a new school year, the conditions can't be any different. While he tries to entice sleep, Hank realizes how foolish he'd been on all those final nights of summer. When he met Eddie on the first day of school, it was as though they never left, and it was never as bad as he thought it would be. The classes were never as difficult as his teachers threatened. Seventh grade wasn't any harder than eighth grade nor was ninth harder than tenth.

Before climbing into bed, Hank packs his bags and places them near his door. He reasons that if all he has to do is get up and leave, there will be less drama. As Hank is memorizing the pattern of cracks in the ceiling above his bed just after dawn, he dozes off. A knock startles him, and his mother's voice indicates that Mr. Durán is outside. Hank quickly washes the sleep away, dresses, and walks downstairs with his two suitcases.

The actual scene is nothing at all like his imagined ones.

His father didn't hatch a plan to keep him home, so there is no screaming or arguing. Stefano isn't even there — he left for work a few hours earlier. The house is eerily quiet.

The only similarity between reality and fantasy is tears. Hank's nonna cries as she hugs her grandson goodbye.

Hank's mother looks at him with her endearing downward smile. She then says, "Angelo, you are not a boy anymore. You become a man today. You doing what you want to do. You the first person in the family to go to college. I'm-a so proud." She kisses him, hugs him, and cries tears of joy.

Ricky Durán gets out of the car when he sees Hank smiling wide and hopping down the stairs with two weightless suitcases. Ricky is stunned at how heavy they are when he loads them in the trunk. Most of the hour ride from Russian Hill to Palo Alto is spent laughing and rehashing stories from the old days, some of which aren't so old. After Ricky Durán parks the car in front of the school, Hank's mentor talks to his borrowed son about grades, making good choices, and his opportunity and potential. Hank will never have to alter this scene in his memory, because it's perfect. He may replay it from different angles or perspectives, but each one will leave him feeling better than the next. If he chooses the point of view from outside the car, his camera will see them sitting in the front seat. Ricky will be talking from the heart, and Hank will nod his head every so often. He will listen intently as he did all those years ago when Ricky Durán gave him his first basketball, some confidence, and a gentle push in the direction of his destiny.

When Ricky drives away, Hank stands, staring at the grandeur of his new home. He has never seen anything like it.

Ricky offers to walk him around, but he respectfully declines. Besides feeling uncomfortable about taking Ricky away from his family on a Sunday, Hank also has the urge to take it all in by himself. He'd planned to visit Stanford on several occasions, but his circumstances caused him to cancel the arrangements. This place is nothing like Russian Hill. He feels as though he'd stepped into a funky time machine and was transported back to the Italian Renaissance, a reckoning which isn't far from the truth.

* * *

MILLIONAIRE REPUBLICAN SENATOR and former California governor, Leland Stanford, and his wife, Jane, opened Stanford University on October 1, 1891. While the difference between 1935 and 1891 is a mere forty-four years, the architectural design of Stanford is much older. The Romanesque style, which developed in Italy and France, dates back to the 6th century. When the Stanfords took a trip to Florence, Italy, their only child, fifteen-year-old Leland junior, was stricken with typhoid and died. Shortly after his burial, the Stanfords converted their 8,200-acre stock farm into an institution for higher education, and Leland Stanford Junior University was dedicated to the memory of their son. America's thirty-first president, Herbert Hoover, was among the inaugural graduating class of Stanford University in 1895.

CHAPTER NINE

HANK LEAVES HIS suitcases with security at the campus entrance and receives directions to the main offices. Since he is one of the last to arrive, he finds the check-in process seamless. He shows his paperwork and signs a few forms, then he is given a key, a welcome folder, and a campus map with directions to his dorm. Hank marvels at the continuous rolling arches encircling the quadrangle. While the arches are classic Romanesque, the buildings are made of thick sandstone walls accented with red Spanish roofs, a design borrowed from the regional decor. The memorial church, the focal point of the quad, is all European. Its colorful mosaic on the front entranceway is a grand image of Jesus teaching and welcoming pilgrims.

The quad is a hive of activity. Some students mosey about, enjoying the lazy afternoon, while others walk like they are on a mission—perhaps some last-minute preparations for the new school year. Most of the population chat in various-sized clusters, eating, hanging out, or sunning themselves. As it is such a gorgeous day, the dorms are empty.

Hank finds his room, inserts the thick, brass key, and enters. As an only child, he isn't used to sharing a room, but he doesn't mind the idea, especially since he was told that they would make every attempt to room athletes of the same sport together. The room is warm and smells of socks, jock straps, fermented T-shirts, and freshly cleaned linens—like former athletes left their stink behind as some sort of hazing ritual. The laundered linens are a feeble attempt by the cleaning crew to mask the scent from the newbies…or to help them get through their chores. Two beds form an L at the back of the rectangular-shaped room. Hank's bed, the one without sheets, is adjacent to and up against a 3 ½ foot high by 4 ½ foot long cast iron radiator — a commodity on cold nights but not much fun if one smashes one's head into it in the middle of a dream.

His roommate's bed is against a wall where he already hung a cardinal red, triangular pennant flag. Stanford is printed in white letters that begin large near the wide end of the flag but reduce in proportion as the pennant narrows to a pointy tip at the opposite end. Running vertically down the large area of the pennant, and before the letter "S," is a picture of an Indian head. This angry, caricature has two white-tipped red feathers, twice as long as his head, sticking straight up. Two thick, red hair ties encircle the ends of each braid dangling on each side of his head. A large, fat, circular nose hangs low, blocking his chin. Large, round, glaring eyes appear under an angry unibrow, and a small grimacing mouth darts to the left. One round ear peaks out of the left side of his head just above the braid.

There's a full-length mirror on the closet door, and all the glass doorknobs, a popular fashion of the times, are made to look like large diamonds.

One of the two sets of drawers has a can of Dinty Moore beef stew on top. Hank thinks if this is representative of university cuisine, he might have a problem. Living in an Italian household and owning a restaurant sets the food bar pretty high.

Hank locates his sheets, folded beneath his pillow in the closet, makes his bed, and unpacks. Just as he finishes, he hears a key twisting in the lock and a tall, muscular boy with curly blond hair enters.

When the boy notices Hank sitting there, he jumps backward, slams his back into the door, and puts his hand on his heart. "Holy crap! You scared the bejesus out of me."

He and Hank laugh as the boy bends over with his hand on his hips, catching his breath.

He straightens and walks over to Hank with an outstretched hand. "You must be Angelo. I'm Bryan Moore. My friends call me Dinty."

"Hello! My friends call me Hank."

They shake.

Hank looks over at the can on the dresser and then back at Dinty. "Let me guess. One of your friends thought it was funny because of the stew, right?"

Dinty smiles with a quick nod. "Something like that. Hey, do you have time for a pick-up game? Some of us are meeting at the outdoor courts."

Hank's eyes widen. "Sure!"

"I just ran in to get my ball." Dinty goes to the closet, gets his ball, and the two dart out.

Dinty dribbles as they walk along a path.

Hank asks, "Are you used to the room smell yet?"

"The room smells?"

Approximately thirty yards away are new basketball courts, and to the right of the courts is a group of boys gathered around a picnic table—every one of them is over six feet tall. The tallest of the group, standing six foot five, is Art Stoefen, who wears new high-end basketball attire. He has perfectly groomed blond hair, an upright posture, and his countenance airs on the side of snobbish and proper, but he's a sweetheart of a guy and a complete gentleman. Jack "Spook" Calderwood has droopy eyes that accent a ghoulish yet slightly goofy look. Black-haired, blue-eyed "Handsome" Howie Turner is shirtless and has the looks and six-pack abs of a cover model. Bobby and Phil Zonne are brothers who, besides being tall, look nothing alike. Bobby is blond haired and freckled with all legs and no torso, while Phil has black hair and olive skin and is more proportionate than his brother. H.B. Lee and Nobbs talk to each other a little to the left of the group. Howie rises when he sees Dinty and Hank walking toward them, and whistles for the ball. Dinty launches it in his direction, but Spook jumps up and steals it. Spook, followed by the pack, minus Nobbs and H.B., runs onto the court and shoots a two-handed set-shot. Rebounding and shots at goal follow.

Those on the court pause when Dinty and Hank arrive, then Nobbs and H.B. stroll over.

Dinty introduces Hank. "Hey guys, this is Hank Luisetti. Hank, this is Art Stoefen, brother of tennis pro, Lester. The beautiful creature to my right is Spook Calderwood. He's from Transylvania."

Laughter comes from all, including Spook.

"Howie Turner is also on the freshmen squad with us. These four, Nobbs, H.B. Lee, and the Zonne brothers—Phil and Bobby—are sophomores."

Nobbs spreads his fingers toward Dinty, indicating that he wants the ball. Dinty tosses it to him, and Nobbs dribbles in place.

Howie studies Hank. "You played for Galileo, right?"

Spook chimes in before Hank could answer. "We called you the crazy kid with the one-handed shot."

Hank smiles.

"I thought you looked familiar, but we didn't play you guys last year," Dinty says.

Nobbs scrunches his eyebrow. "One hand? That I have to see, frosh!" He passes to Hank, who bounces the ball once, then swishes a one-hander. Nobbs looks at H.B. and back at Hank. "That was pretty damned good!"

Phil Zonne adds, "Smooth."

Howie picks up the ball and positions himself for a shot. "Like this?"

Hank demonstrates the one-handed position for Howie. "That's about right, but a little lighter touch with your bottom hand. You use it to steady the ball, not hold it."

Walking up from behind are John Bunn and Dr. Elliot. The group is so focused on Hank that the two men go unnoticed. Howie shoots but the ball sails two feet over the backboard.

"May want to ease up a tad, Howell," says Bunn.

The boys turn around.

"Good afternoon. I'd like to introduce you all to Dr. Richard Elliot, president of this great institution."

Dr. Elliot waves, "Greetings, boys!"

The boys wave politely and smile at the two men. Spook shakes Dr. Elliot's hand.

"Dr. Elliot brought me here to win championships, and I told him we're gonna play a brand of basketball that's new to most of you… and your opponents. Ball control offense and man-to-man defense are out! On the attack, we'll switch positions to meet developing situations."

Hank listens carefully.

Bunn uses hand gestures as he speaks. "Dinty here might play the post, bring the ball down, or switch from left to right at will. You'll have the freedom to pop that pill in from anywhere. We'll play what I call, team defense—a combination of zone and man to man."

The varsity boys look at each other and at Bunn incredulously.

"I have been at the helm of the movement to eliminate the center jump following each basket for quite some time now, and I'm proud to say that the West will be the first region in the nation to make this change, which goes into effect at the start of the season. This innovation will quicken the game's pace and make it more of a ride instead of a start/stop traffic jam. My new playing strategy gels with this new phase of the game, and I'm excited to see it all come together in real time."

Hank's mind races with thoughts of how this new pace will add gasoline to the fire of his one-handed mindset.

Bunn hooks his thumbs into his waistband and says, "For the moment, though, just have some fun. I didn't mean to interrupt."

The boys politely dismiss themselves and jog toward the court. Bunn and Elliot walk to a picnic table and sit.

"I'm building this team around talented, free-spirited athletes," Bunn says.

Hank spins around Dinty and hook-passes to Spook.

Elliot points to Hank. "That boy's good." Hank rebounds and scores a layup. "Very good."

"The best one out there by far, but he does, however, come with a serious flaw."

Elliot angles his head in the manner of a curious puppy.

Bunn continues, "He's completely devoid of hubris."

* * *

HANK'S NEW FRIENDS are intrigued with his unorthodox playing style, so after the varsity players leave, Hank teaches his new teammates the fundamentals of the one-hander and how it removes the chains of the stop-set-shoot mindset. They all take to it remarkably well, especially Dinty. The two become fast friends and host Spook, Howie, and Art in their room that night where they all get to know each other, but the focus is clearly on Hank. Not only is he the newest member of the squad, but they admire his athletic prowess. After Howie, Spook, and Art leave, Hank and Dinty stay up talking well into the night.

Hank receives a message from Coach Bunn the next morning, asking to meet that afternoon. He asks Dinty if Bunn met with him, but he hadn't. As far as Dinty knows, Bunn hasn't met privately with anyone on the team. Hank has only been at Stanford one day, and he's already on the wrong side of the coach. It dawns on him that it must have something to do with him teaching his teammates the one-hander. Apparently, Bunn found out and wants to set Hank straight about who the teacher is.

Hank arrives at Coach Bunn's office at precisely four o'clock. He actually got there a half hour early but waited outside the building until 3:55 p.m., so he could demonstrate professionalism.

Hank knocks on the door.

"It's open," Bunn says.

Bunn's small office is stuffed with a large, messy desk, two tall file cabinets, and an old chair with cracks in its green upholstery. The low ceiling makes it a claustrophobe's nightmare. Bunn does not look at Hank for a few seconds as he's writing on a yellow legal pad, and doesn't raise his head until he pops a period on the paper and drops his pencil on the desk. He looks up at Hank and points to the chair.

"Please, have a seat."

"Thank you." Hank folds his hands, then quickly puts

them on his thighs and slides them up and down a few times in an attempt to iron out nervous energy.

Bunn asks, "How's everything so far?"

"Great!"

"Good. Very good." Bunn leans back in the chair and rubs his chin.

Hank bites his lip and is on the verge of promising not to teach anyone anything anymore when Bunn begins talking.

"You have the best moves, and, without a doubt, the best shot I've ever seen—and son, I've been around a while. But you only averaged five points a game at Galileo. That just doesn't add up."

"Sir, I'm a play-maker. I work the ball to the open man closest to the basket."

Bunn leans back in his chair and folds his hands on his stomach. "You look for the open man when you're the man who's open, and you pass to guys who can't shoot nearly as well as you. Now that might be polite, but it ain't smart basketball. You can't be a floorwalker if you want to remain on my team."

An electric spark tap dances up Hank's spine.

Bunn leans forward. "My orders are simple. Stop holding on to that apple and shoot!" He pauses a moment, letting these next words register. "Mr. Durán would have a championship banner hanging at Galileo if you hadn't passed off to a guy who's probably working in a food market right now. The Good Lord endowed you with an abundance of talent, and from this moment on, I want to see you honor that gift. Scoring points wins basketball games, son." Bunn pauses for a few beats and then smiles.

Hank sprouts a boyish grin. "I'll do my best, sir."

"Good, because I'm counting on you."

* * *

THE CARTOONIST IS busy at work. The drawing grows to include an Indian holding an axe. The Indian stands near the horse and looks at the tree. The artist takes a pack of Camels from his top pocket, shakes out a cigarette, and grabs it with his lips. He grasps a lighter off the desk, pops it open with one flick of his thumb, and reverses direction swiping the flint wheel downward. A white spark sets off a generous blue and orange flame. He tilts his head, sticks the cigarette into the flame, sucks in, and snaps the lighter closed with a flick of his wrist—a practiced routine. He takes a deep, quick drag, puts the cigarette in the ashtray, picks up his pencil, and places it in the branches of the tree.

CHAPTER TEN

NED IRISH STANDS in the center of four men wearing dark suits. They are behind podiums, draped with college banners along the half court line of Madison Square Garden. The man to his right, in his late thirties, is Clair Bee; he stands behind the Long Island University banner. To Irish's left is a dapper-looking man also in his late thirties. He has black hair and wears a three-piece suit. He's Nat Holman from City College; CCNY appears on his banner. Howard Cann is from NYU, and Buck Freeman is from St. John's University. A dozen news reporters snap photos and jot notes.

Irish raises one hand and waits for silence. A student from CCNY's school newspaper, fussing with his camera, doesn't notice. Ned eyeballs him until the reporter next to the college kid elbows him and jerks his eyebrows in Irish's direction. Now the reddened boy focuses on the stage.

Irish turns from the reporter to the crowd. "Tonight begins a new era."

Reporters jot notes.

"Gone are the days when this great sport is hidden in armories and dance halls. From this moment forward, Madison Square Garden will be its main venue and the vehicle by which this era begins. It's fitting, though, since our local teams have earned the reputation as the class of the nation, and each of you standing with me is responsible for that. From the veteran Nat Holman..."

Holman closes his eyes and gives a quick nod.

"...to Clair Bee and his boys from LIU, the number-one

ranked team in the nation—a team so respected, they were asked to represent the United States at the summer Olympic Games in Berlin. They refused, however, as a sign of protest due to reports of anti-Semitic activities in Hitler's Nazi Germany."

Flashbulbs pop all around.

Irish looks to his right—a silent clue indicating that Clair Bee should respond.

At first, Clair smiles and nods his head as Nat Holman did a minute ago, but when Irish continues his blank stare, Bee understands and speaks. "Thank you, Ned. New York has gained notoriety because we respect the game's integrity, yet there are those who are taking liberties and tampering with its very essence. In New York, however, we will continue to adhere to the highest standard, and we will continue to be the breeding ground for basketball's thrilling future."

The sparkles and smoke from bursting flashbulbs replicate a mini firework display as the audience applauds. Irish smiles politely and professionally, beads of sweat sit high on his forehead.

* * *

ACROSS THE COUNTRY, at the half-filled Stanford Pavilion, two teams warm-up on either end of the court. The Stanford Indians' uniform consists of a cardinal red tank top jersey with white piping along the neck and shoulders. The sparse, satin European style trunks are of the same style as the ones worn at Galileo. The shorts continue the white piping accent. Hank's number seven is displayed on the front and back of his jersey. The UCLA Bruins' uniform is a blue and white version of Stanford's.

MADNESS

Dr. Elliot speaks into a microphone at center court. "Welcome to the opening game of the freshman basketball season."

Applause, like the initial sporadic pops of heating popcorn, mock the event.

"One week from tonight, right here in the Pavilion, is the freshman basketball dance. Food, drinks, and live music from the Stanford swing band will ensure a good time for all. Thank you for your support." Dr. Elliot begins clapping and is joined by a few faithfuls from the sleepy crowd.

A boy wearing oversized black-framed glasses, grips a camera around his neck as he walks with a bouncy step along the sideline; he is Miles Lee. Lee has short, blond, combed over hair, high-water pants, and a checkered sport jacket. He stops in front of John Bunn, who is studying his players' warm-up drills.

Bunn joins his middle finger and thumb, presses it into his tongue, and whistles. The Indians stop and turn toward their coach. "Run drill three!"

Miles takes a pad and pencil from the inner pocket of his jacket and pushes his glasses up with his index finger. "Mr. Bunn..."

Bunn glances at Lee and then looks to the court. "What can I do for you, young man?"

"I'm Miles Lee, reporter for the Stanford Daily."

"The who?"

"The school newspaper."

Bunn gives him another quick glance before he swings his attention back to the court. "That's nice."

Miles understands that Bunn's not interested in talking, and he walks off. When he gets ten feet away, he kneels and snaps a photo of the Stanford coach. Bunn doesn't flinch as he's fixed on Howie.

Howie misses a one-handed shot from the foul line, and he approaches Hank. "Does this ever happen to you? I was sinking them yesterday."

Four Bruins watch Hank position Howie for the shot. Howie shoots and misses. Art attempts a one-hander and misses as well.

The Bruins laugh, and one of them honks like a goose in between machine gun guffaws. The Honker chokes out, "Look at those weirdos," as he cracks himself up.

Bunn grimaces just before a squealing whistle sends him his players.

The Stanford team gathers round Bunn in a semicircle. He clears his throat before saying, "We're gonna build a legacy at Stanford, and it starts right now! The elimination of the center jump and the addition of our style of play will make history this year. Show this half-filled arena what you're made of, and the next time we play, this place'll be filled. The time after that, we'll be turning 'em away. Go out there and hit 'em with all you've got!"

The team claps before the starters roll onto the court, and the reserves go toward the bench.

Bunn grabs Hank's arm as the starters jog off. "Sic 'em, kid!"

Hank gives a quick nod and follows his teammates.

The referee tosses up the ball for a center jump, and Art taps it to Hank who dribbles away. He passes to Howie, who shoots an offline, one-handed air ball.

Honker shouts, "Nice shot!"

The Bruins' center pulls it down, dribbles, and passes to Honker. Hank tips the ball in midair, lunges forward, and takes control while on the run. He drives toward the goal, weaving around players like they are staked structures on an obstacle course. Hank finds his spot and shoots a silky-smooth twenty-five-foot one-hander that whooshes through. Miles catches the moment with a pop of his flashbulb. Honker is in the background, openmouthed.

* * *

WHILE HANK WAS given orders to shoot at will, it isn't his nature to play that way. He battles the Bruins and his moral compass; modesty is a part of the cast-iron identity he's forged throughout his life. He gets a thrill out of passing off, so others have a chance to shine. He reasons that his Stanford teammates are not high schoolers. They are far better than his friends at Galileo, so why shouldn't he pass to them? Basketball isn't tennis or bowling or golf—it's a team sport. After his first goal, Hank falls into his familiar pattern as a playmaker. Most of the game, Stanford is up by two points, but it requires consistent effort.

Hank harbors one philosophy and Bunn another, so the coach benches him after the second quarter. UCLA immediately goes up by four points and holds onto the lead. Four points become eight, and Hank watches helplessly from the bench. He knows his coach pulled him for not following orders, but Bunn's reasoning doesn't sink in until Hank sees the game from a different angle. His team isn't much different without him. They are better with him but not by much, and Bunn said what Hank knew all along—Galileo would have won if he'd listened to Ricky Durán. Bunn is not as forgiving as Ricky, however. He doesn't look at Hank and see a kid with leg braces who grew up under his tutelage.

Hank is itching to get back in, but he isn't sure if he'll get the chance. With the game slipping away, Bunn gives him the nod midway through the fourth quarter, and Hank never looks back. He shoots when he feels he can score instead of seeking an open man. It speeds up his game, and he finds it liberating. Hank sinks four unanswered goals which ties the score. The more he shoots, the more he enjoys the rise of the crowd, the thrill of his teammates, and the competitive beast that grows inside him. The beast has always been there, but John Bunn unlocked the cage. By the time it's over, the Indians win their home opener, Hank scores twenty-four points, and John Bunn has his star.

* * *

THE NEXT DAY, Dinty is standing on a chair in his room, holding a hammer, and Hank hands him a newspaper page. Dinty reaches in his pocket and jerks it out as if he were bitten.

"Crap!" Dinty shakes his hand a few times and then examines the tip of his index finger.

Hank belly laughs.

"Damn, that hurt!" Dinty carefully reaches into his pocket and takes out a thumbtack.

Hank continues laughing as Dinty proceeds to attach the newspaper to the wall above his bed, just to the right of the Stanford Indian pennant. The paper reads, "Freshmen Squad Tames UCLA in Opener. Luisetti Scores 24." Dinty plops on the chair to admire his handiwork, but he shoots straight up off the thumbtack strategically placed by Hank.

"Ouch! Crap! That's not funny, Hank!" Dinty sticks his hand down the rear of his pants, pulls it out, and looks at his finger. "It's bleeding!"

Hank laughs even harder and crumples onto the bed.

Dinty shakes his head and chuckles too. "You're an ass!"

MADNESS

That weekend, a giant red banner with white lettering announcing the Second Annual Freshmen Basketball Dance is draped across the ceiling of the Pavilion. Couples dance the Lindy as musicians, wearing red jackets and bow ties above white shirts and pants, play trumpets, trombones, saxophones, as well as a drum and one bass fiddle. Hank, Dinty, Nobbs, Art, H.B., Bobby, and Phil, in jackets and ties, are gathered together talking. A few of them hold cups. Howie stands fifteen feet from the group, talking to a striking blonde. A chunky girl with a large pink bow on her head stands near Howie, but she is talking to Spook. Dinty crawls on his hands and knees behind a row of chairs directly behind Spook, and when Spook and the girl look in opposite directions, he reaches up, pats Spook's butt, and pulls his hand back. Spook looks at the girl and smiles. The girl smiles and turns her head, coyly, so Spook reaches over and pinches her behind. She looks at Spook in horror, smacks him in the car, then stomps over to Howie's girl and tells her what happened. The two girls storm off. Spook looks at Howie and shrugs while Hank and his friends howl.

Weeks later, Dinty and Hank are in their dorm wearing coats. Dinty holds a hammer as they look at the scrapbook wall that now spans four across. The newest three are:

Cal Crushed by Freshmen 32 - 15. Luisetti Disproves Luck Theory - Scores 20!

Freshmen Win a Laugher at Santa Clara.

Luisetti's 26 Downs Trojans.

Two rectangular, brass-buckled suitcases, one brown and one blue, are near the door.

Spook, wearing a large Santa hat, swings open the door. "If you guys want a ride, you'd better get your behinds downstairs!"

"All right already!" Dinty grabs the chair and puts it in its place by the desk. He then picks up a suitcase, nabs the Santa hat off Spook's head, and runs out.

Spook takes off after him.

Hank beams as he gives the wall one last look before picking up his suitcase and walking out the door.

CHAPTER ELEVEN

EVEN THOUGH HANK lives a stone's throw from Stanford, for obvious reasons, he doesn't go back home until Christmas. He calls home once a week and speaks to his mother and grandmother, both of whom ask the same three questions: if he's eating enough, if he feels sick, and how he's doing in school—in that order. Hank comes home a day earlier than he told his mother. He figures it's a nice surprise, but he mostly wants to get home while his parents are at work so he can avoid any potential confrontations.

Hank drops off his bags and takes a trolley to the City of Paris store to do Christmas shopping. For his father, he buys a white, button-down shirt even though he is certain he wouldn't wear it. Hank thinks buying pajamas for his grandmother and mother is a good idea until he finds himself wandering the women's department as the sole male. On his way out, he notices a slipper display, standing between a rack of bras on one side and a panty bin on the other. He grabs a slipper from the display and turns it around in his hand until a voice startles him.

"Still wearing girls' undies, Hank?"

He turns to see Connie D'Angelo looking more gorgeous than ever. Her long black hair flows from her red cloche hat and blankets her shoulders. She wears a mid-length red jacket with a black belt, and everything is tied together by her signature red lips.

Hank, as red as Connie's lips, spurts out, "Connie... Hi! Oh... no... I'm... looking at these slippers." He swings his arm around and knocks over the display. They both laugh and pick up the merchandise. Hank gets flushed by waves of heat.

"Nice shot, Hank!"

His synthetic laugh catches in his throat and sends a blast of hot chili peppers straight to his already glowing ears.

Connie switches gears. "How's college?"

"Great!"

"You're playing basketball, right?" she asks, stuffing a slipper into the display.

"Yeah, we're undefeated so far."

"How could they lose with you on the team?"

"I don't know about that. I can be pretty clumsy, you know."

Connie hands him the last slipper, and he tucks it in.

A young man holding a shopping bag with a groomed mustache and a tailored suit, approaches Connie.

Connie smiles at him and extends her arm toward Hank. "Gerard, this is Hank Luisetti. We went to high school together."

Hank puts out his hand. "Nice to meet you."

They shake, and Gerard's knuckles crackle under Hank's grip.

Gerard says, "Same here." He turns to Connie. "Ready, darling?"

Connie nods and looks at Hank. "It was nice to see you, Hank... Merry Christmas!"

"Merry Christmas, Connie!"

They walk away, but she stops at a nearby hat display. Reaching for one, she glances at Hank from the side of her sleepy green eyes and holds him under a spell before releasing him with a brush of her long black lashes. She puts the hat back and strolls off with Gerard.

Hank keeps a fixed eye on Connie for a few beats, then takes a step backward and knocks over the slippers again.

* * *

THE MOST CELEBRATED holiday for Italian-Americans is Christmas Eve or La Vigilia (The Vigil)—the night of the seven fishes. Italians have different variations of this feast, and it's determined by family tradition. Some Italians cook seven courses while others choose twelve in honor of the apostles, but seven is the most common denomination. The fish, too, depends on tradition, but some of the popular varieties are Baccalà or salted cod, calamari, shrimp, anchovies, clams, mussels, lobster, crab, and flounder. While some serve each fish as separate courses, some prepare a mixture of seafood in a marinara sauce and let it cook in a pot of tomato sauce, olive oil, garlic, salt, and basil—plus crushed red pepper flakes if it's a Fra Diavolo sauce. They let it simmer for hours before pouring it over hot linguini, al dente of course. Before the fish, there's always antipasto, an appetizer consisting of cured meats such as salami, prosciutto, mortadella, etc.; cheeses like mozzarella or provolone; artichoke hearts; pickled meats or vegetables such as red peppers and olives; and mushrooms. There is also a hot variety consisting of miniature Italian entrées, which features fried foods and melted mozzarella. After the fish, there are nuts, fruit, and of course, homemade desserts and espresso in miniature, colorful cups with tiny brass-colored spoons.

While this revered tradition is a staple for most Italians, it is not celebrated in the Luisetti household on Christmas Eve, as the fish store and restaurant are mobbed on that day. The

Luisettis usually postpone this feast until the following Monday. While the restaurant is open on the twenty-fourth, it's closed on the twenty-fifth, and the Luisettis exchange hugs, kisses, and gifts, while they play Christmas music and drink *cioccolata calda con panna* or what's commonly known in America as hot cocoa with dollops of homemade whipped cream.

The scene is very different on Hank's first visit from Stanford, however, since Stefano will not partake in the gift-giving tradition, claiming that he is "too busy" preparing the Christmas meal. Stefano's absence, as well as the question of whether he will eat with his family, become the two-ton elephant they tip toe around as they feign happiness during the gift-giving charade. They initially breathe a sigh of relief when the elephant sits down to dinner; however, it speaks to no one and its stillness silences everyone. Once the main course is over, it clears the table and spends the remainder of the evening washing dishes. A roll of Italian expletives follows the shattering of glass, but no one knows if it is thrown in anger or if it slips away from soapy fingers. No matter what is happening between father and son, Carmela will not allow it to ruin the highlight of her evening—scopa, an Italian card game that many Italian Americans refer to as scobe.

Hank and Amalia sit across from each other with Carmela at the head. Each of the trio holds a fist of cards and has a pile of pennies before them. Another pile of pennies sits in the center of the table near a fruit bowl. A Christmas tree with an angel topper flashes colored lights on the table from across the room. Opera plays softly from a Victrola and flavors the air with the sounds of Italy. Hank jumps up to answer the phone located on a small table. The phone is vertical, like a candlestick, and has a cone-like mouthpiece positioned at the top. The weighted base is topped with a rotary dial, and an earpiece that looks like a fat Lincoln log is held to a person's ear during the call.

Hank picks up the phone. "Hello… Eddie?"

The call is from Eddie Kinsman stationed in Manila. He wears green pants and a khaki T-shirt, and his hair is buzzed short on top with bald sides. A blue ink bulldog, standing above the letters USMC, is tattooed on his right bicep, which is rounder and larger than it was when he left home. Eddie's phone resembles Hank's, but the body is rectangular and has three coin slots on top, sized for quarters, nickels, and dimes. There are some coins on a shelf near the bottom of the phone.

Eddie speaks with vigor. "I'm doing great! It's paradise, Hank!"

Hank asks, "What was that?"

Eddie talks, but fizzy static muffles his words.

Carmela shouts out, "Tell him to call-a later!"

Amalia talks into the phone, "Buon Natale, Eddie!"

"Bony tally, Mrs. Luisetti."

The operator says, "Please deposit three dollars for the next one minute."

"Three dollars?" Eddie exclaims.

The operator repeats "Three dollars for the next one minute, please."

"Give me a break, operator. I'm defending America's liberties overseas… Hey Hank, how's Stanford? Did your dad speak to you yet?"

"It's great… We still haven't spoken, but we ate at the same table. It's a start. Hey, you'll never guess who I met."

The operator interrupts, "Three dollars, please."

"You're annoying, lady!" Eddie says.

Hank hears a click. "Eddie? Hello?" He hangs up and

walks back to the table. "He called all the way from Manila."

Carmela frowns. "Sit down and-a let's finish."

Hank smiles, shakes his head at his nonna, and sits. He and Amalia reacquaint themselves with their cards. Hank throws down a card then Amalia throws one down.

Carmela squeals, "Scopa! Hahaha!" She rubs her palms together, like a mouse, before gathering the penny pot with both hands. She counts the coins in twos, "Due, quattro, sei—"

A knock on the front door springs Amalia from her seat. "We have-a company!" she says as she rushes out of the room.

"Hey, there's-a one penny short!" Carmela steals a penny from Amalia's pile as she gets up to greet the company. She looks at her penny pile and then warns Hank with her signature chopping motion.

After Carmela leaves, Hank chuckles as he takes a penny out of her pile and puts it on the floor. Stefano chills the air as he struts by like a horse with blinders.

Hank delivers his rehearsed line. "Do you need any help at the restaurant? I'll be home for a few weeks."

Stefano speaks with a raised chin, "I have enough-a help, thank you."

Dante, a man in his thirties with a mustache that looks like he has a small brush velcroed to his upper lip, backs Stefano into the room. He's wearing a suit and holds a white bakery box tied with thin candy-cane colored string.

"Buon Natale, Stefano!" Dante says.

Hank looks blankly at Stefano as his father enthusiastically greets Dante.

Dante and Stefano kiss each other on both cheeks, a traditional European greeting.

Afterward, Dante notices Hank. "Ah! Angelo! Buon Natale! Buon Natale! It's-a so nice to see you again!"

Hank rises and they greet each other European style. Amalia, Carmela, Dante's wife Maria, and his four young children file into the room.

Hank excuses himself.

Amalia's doleful eyes trail her son as he leaves. She turns her attention to Stefano just long enough for him to notice her fiery gaze. Amalia then turns to her guests and asks cheerfully, "Who would like something to eat?"

A joyful concerto begins playing from the Victrola and adds another layer to the thin facade of blinking lights, glittery garland, good food, card games, and happiness.

CHAPTER TWELVE

THE HOLIDAYS COME and go without change. Hank spends his time reading and playing basketball in the park. He got a book list from his English professor and decides to read the required texts while he is home so he can focus on basketball when he returns. Amalia works exclusively at the fish store while her son is home because it closes at six, and she can make dinner for Hank at night. This is a special treat for him, especially after eating cafeteria food for four months. The Stanford selection is not bad, but no one cooks like Amalia... or the restaurant for that matter. Hank helps his mom cook, as he is trained in every aspect of the restaurant business. He and his mother cook and eat together, play cards together, and talk together. Hank has always had a good relationship with Amalia, but their bond grows deeper because of the family feud and because of guilt — Hank's for not taking over the restaurant and Amalia's for failing to prevent the war between the two men she loves most.

Expectations, conditions, guilt, and pride are the all-too-common compounds that befall many families. Love fuels the firestorm. Many refuse to see love as anything other than blissfulness, but love wears two masks. Its happiness is the climax of human emotion, but it's a twin peak because the pain of a broken heart is just as potent. In the case of feuding relationships, the intensity of love between people coincides with the severity of the resulting wounds. While war plagues the Luisetti home, the time spent between mother and son is a remedy of sorts, a salve, even though each fear the bitterness will not end for many years… or at all.

* * *

RICKY DURÁN INVITES Hank to watch the Lions' home opener. It feels strange going back to Galileo. He spent the past four years of his life there, and while he was a student and an athlete, it felt like home. When he walks the halls this night, however, he realizes it is more like a rented apartment, and a new crop of tenants have taken over the place. Hank walks into the gym and cringes to find the resident warden, Miss. Fogarty, otherwise known as Old Fogerty or Old Fartery, sitting at the admission table with her handmade 10¢ price-of-admission sign. She is a robust woman in her late sixties, wearing a paisley dress with her gray hair nesting in a bun at the top of her head. Students heard three things about Fogarty:

She's been teaching English at Galileo since the Jurassic Period.

She lives in catacombs beneath the school.

She is such a tough grader that Shakespeare would have been lucky to get a B in her class.

Hank never had her as a teacher, but she made him uncomfortable. She knew him by name, which he found odd, and greeted him in the halls with, "Hello, Mr. Luisetti." Yet it was never a pleasant hello; instead, it was as if she knew something about him and was biding her time before producing the evidence. Her hello was more like "I have my eye on you." He thought she was so weird.

There are a few students in line ahead of Hank, and Old Fogarty greets them with a stern look. After taking their money, she follows them with a hawk-like stare until they feel her gaze and turn to look at her. When she turns toward the next inmate, her rigid, V-shaped eyebrows invert into semicircles of joy. She gasps like a grandmother seeing her grandson, "Angelo! Oh my! It's so nice to see you. How are you?" Before he can answer, she asks, "How's Stanford? You know I graduated from there many years ago."

Hank blinks a few times, taking it all in and wondering if she finally snapped after a lifetime of negativity. He manages to get out, "Everything's great... I didn't know you went to Stanford."

"Yes, that was many years ago. I would tell you the year I graduated, but you might be shocked."

Hank thinks, I'm sure I wouldn't be, but breaks the awkward silence by reaching into his pocket to retrieve his dime.

Fogarty shakes her head. "Oh no, Angelo. Your money is no good here. I'll cover your admission price." She opens her purse, flicks through the change with her pointer finger, retrieves a dime, and places it in the coin jar.

"Thank you, Miss. Fogarty."

"You are so welcome, Angelo!" Fogarty watches Hank with Amalia's downward type grin, then scowls at the next victim in line.

Hank reasons that Miss. Fogarty isn't a bad person but was forced to create an offensive persona for her own protection after dealing with thousands of other people's kids for the past umpteen years. He thinks, Wonders will never cease.

He gets a buzz as he walks onto his not-so-old stomping ground with its familiar sights of fans bustling about the bleachers, smells of gymnasium, and the sounds of squeaking sneakers and cheerleaders. Ricky Durán is on the foul line talking to his team as they take turns shooting underhanded foul shots. Two are under the basket rebounding. Mac, Mario, and Yang are this year's seniors.

Yang is the first to see Hank. "Hey look who dropped in!"

Ricky looks up. "There he is. The man from Stanford!"

Hank is enthusiastically greeted with handshakes and celebratory punches.

Ricky tosses a ball to him "Let's see if you still have it."

Hank eyes the basket and holds the ball waist high. Just before he releases it, he hears a familiar voice.

"You call these straight lines?"

Hank turns to see Connie from behind, shouting orders at the cheerleaders. Hank turns, shoots, and sinks it. His friends clap.

Ricky says, "Of course he still has it!"

"It's all because of you, Coach!" Hank turns to the team. "I came here tonight to see you win, so don't disappoint me!"

The team collectively responds in different varieties about how they are going to destroy the Dons.

"I'll be watching," Hank says as he walks away, moving furtively behind Connie.

She points at a girl in the front row. "Maureen, take a half step toward Susan." When she notices that her girls' attention is focused beyond her, she snaps, "Excuse me girls, but I don't care what's going on over there or which boy is cute. Keep your focus on—"

Hank leans his head near Connie's ear. "Is she always this grouchy?"

Connie leaps forward. "Ahh!"

Her girls burst out laughing.

"Hank! Oh my God! What are you doing here? You scared me half to death." She points to the laughing cheerleaders. "And look what you did to my girls."

Hank laughs, and Connie contorts her mouth to keep

from smiling, but she loses the battle.

"I guess I had that coming, huh?"

Hank nods. "Yes, you did." He runs his hand through his hair. "I thought I'd visit Galileo before I left."

She looks at the cheerleaders, claps a few times, and assumes her leadership role. "Okay the fun is over. Run routines one through five. Take over, Betty."

A tall blonde steps forward, claps twice, and shouts, "Here we go, Lions. Here we go!"

Connie leads Hank a few feet away.

He puts his hands in his pockets and says, "I didn't know you coached."

"I fit it in around my job at the pharmacy. I really like it. Are you staying for the whole game?"

Hank nods.

"Great, we'll talk afterwards? I'd love to catch up."

Hank smiles. "Me too."

Connie leaves Hank with one of her cute, flirtatious smiles and saunters away.

* * *

HANK MEETS CONNIE after Galileo's home-opening defeat, and as fate would have it, Gerard's car won't start. So Hank offers to escort her home.

They talk fast and walk slow, and Hank's shy nature melts under Connie's warmth and charm. He has never felt this type of energy exchange with another human being, and every now and again some type of sweet, flowery scent wafts by. He thinks it must be perfume. Whatever it is, it blends with her essence and is the most pleasant scent he has ever experienced. It is like some kind of hypnotic spell that energizes him every time it floats by. Hank always marveled at Connie's beauty, but this is the longest he has ever looked at her. There is something extraordinary about the way she looks this night.

He talks incessantly in order to prevent a gap in their conversation. He goes from the Miss Fogarty experience, to high school, to childhood stories about him and Eddie, to college anecdotes. Hank doesn't know where she lives, but the thought of a final destination makes him walk slower and slower until they are more stationary than moving. Connie speaks too. It is as though they saved several years of conversations for this night. The one subject Connie doesn't mention is the same one Hank is most afraid to discuss—Gerard. But he finally finds the nerve.

"How long have you been with that guy?" Playing it cool, he adds, "Gerard is it?"

"Gerard?" She plays it just as cool. "We go out once in a while. It's not steady or anything."

Hank is slightly relieved.

Connie points. "It's this one."

They stop in front of a detached three-story on a corner lot with a fence and professionally trimmed landscaping. A new Cadillac convertible with fat white walls is parked on a driveway outside the garage. It's the nicest home he'd ever seen.

Hank, still digesting Gerard, spaces out for a beat, and then looks at Connie who's looking at him. It's his turn to speak, but a dam formed in his throat when they stopped moving, and the words crashed forward and became lodged in his voice box. He ponders the urge to kiss her as her plush green eyes sing a siren's song. The hesitation costs him.

Connie breaks the silence. "It was great catching up and

really sweet of you to walk me home."

"Any time... Well, I mean, if I lived here... You know what I mean... Do you know what I mean?" he bumbles.

"I know what you mean."

"That makes one of us, because I have no idea what the heck I'm talking about."

They laugh—not because it's amusing but because they are experiencing that unique phase when young love could make anything funny, cute, or endearing.

Connie takes a pen out of her pocketbook, tears a piece of paper from something buried in there, scribbles on it, and hands it to Hank. "Don't be a stranger."

Hank takes the paper, and he and Connie stand there staring at each other. This hesitation also costs him as Connie turns and walks the path to her front door.

Hank watches her, mesmerized, and thinks, Even her walk is amazing.

Just before she goes in, Connie turns to him and waves. Hank waves back, and she vanishes. He looks at the piece of paper, folds it, and places it in his jacket pocket.

Seconds later, it seems, he approaches his front door, remembering nothing along the way. It was as though he had fallen asleep in front of Connie's house and woken up in front of his. He thinks about the kiss that didn't happen. God! How can anyone look that perfect, walk that perfect, and smell... smell... that prefect? What was that smell? People don't smell that way. Then he chuckles and says, "It's either I've been spending too much time in my stinking dorm, or I might have just walked an angel home."

CHAPTER THIRTEEN

A WEEK LATER, Hank sits on his bed holding Connie's number. Dinty sits on his right, and Spook on his left. Howie and Art sit in front of him.

Hank snaps his fingers. "What about the game on Saturday?"

Dinty says, "That's good."

Art nods his head. "Yeah."

Howie adds, "Perfect."

"If she's as beautiful as you say she is, I'll call her if you don't," Spook says.

* * *

ON RUSSIAN HILL, Connie—whose actual name is Concetta—sits in her spacious dining room with her four sisters Jelsemina, Lorella, Gisella, Serafina; her nonna, Domenica; her mother, Rosaria; and her father, Joseph. Joseph is a gentleman wearing a three-piece suit, smoking a pipe, and reading a book in a tapestry chair at the far end of the room beside an ornate fireplace.

While Connie's family is similar to Hank's regarding tradition—a nonna who lives with them, and a mother who was born in Italy—their fathers are from different worlds. Joseph D'Angelo is a third-generation Italian American who speaks four languages. Connie's grandfather, John, was a successful executive in the railroad industry, and he made sure his only son was both well-educated and well-traveled. As a child,

Joseph visited every major city in the United States by train and spent his summers in Europe. When he graduated college, he vacationed in Sorrento, Italy with relatives who owned olive and lemon farms.

While sitting in a cafe on the Amalfi Coast, Joseph met and fell in love with the most beautiful woman he'd ever seen—Connie's mother Rosaria, a woman of eighteen who was visiting from the small southern town of Benevento. They were married three months later. Joseph returned to the States and procured a managerial position with the Union Pacific Railroad and quickly worked his way up the corporate ladder. After the San Francisco International Airport opened in 1927, he is offered a prominent position with Pan American Airlines, a career that has him flying around the world in the company plane.

Joseph dotes on his children as much as his schedule permits, but his demanding career in the budding airline industry dictates long hours and frequent business trips. Connie adores her father and his absence weighs on her. She fantasizes about a father who plays with her, goes on picnics, and eats dinner with the family. When Joseph is home he stays close to his children, even if they are engaged in an activity such as they are on this particular evening. He is reading Dickens while his girls sit around the table sewing ribbons and beads onto cheerleader outfits. They listen to Jack Benny, a popular radio personality of the time, from a large wooden radio with four knobs and a speaker covered with gold-speckled cloth.

Jack Benny asks his butler, Rochester, where his slippers are.

Rochester's raspy voice answers, "On my feet."

Everyone except Domenica laughs. The phone rings, and

Serafina, Connie's ten-year-old sister, pops up and disappears behind a bedroom door in an adjacent room.

Jack Benny asks, "Why are they on your feet?"

"It's cold in here!" Rochester replies.

Serafina calls out, "Connie!"

She places her scissors down and walks toward the bedroom. Laughter rings out from both the radio and the D'Angelo family, and Connie chuckles as she enters the room.

Serafina has a hand covering the phone's mouthpiece. She looks at Connie with playful, half-moon eyes, and sings more than says, "Who's Hank Luisetti?"

Connie grasps the phone then shoos her sister out of the room. She fixes her hair, grabs the phone off the nightstand, and talks in a half whisper into the mouthpiece. "Hank? Hi... I'm okay, how about you?" She looks to the door and then back at the phone. "Saturday? Sure, I'd love to." Connie listens to the phone and smiles. "I can take a train... I'm a big girl..." She chuckles. "I'm sure... Buh-bye." She hangs up the phone, shimmies excitedly, and walks out the door.

Dinty, Spook, Art, and Howie are gathered outside a phone booth, peering in at Hank, who flashes the thumbs up before flinging open the accordion door and jumping high in the air. The guys congratulate him as though he just sunk the winning basket of a championship game.

* * *

HANK WAITS SIX days before his date with Connie, during which he lives on a steady stream of adrenaline. He springs out of bed in the morning and goes about his day with cheerful enthusiasm. Things that normally annoy him, such as cafeteria lines, his 8:00 a.m. math class, and Dr. Boring—his real name—a history professor who lectures for the entire class because he loves listening to himself, do not alter Hank's mood. At practices, no one can keep up with him. His reflexes and mind work together in perfect harmony. At one point, Hank jumps so high and stays up so long, Dinty swears that he defies gravity.

When his date with Connie finally arrives, Hank's adrenaline punches up a few notches, yet he is confident and calm. He plans the day from the moment she steps off the train until he brings her back that evening. Hank is waiting at the station when Connie arrives in Palo Alto. He borrows Art's car and takes her to an early dinner. Then they go back to the dorm to meet the boys who are all slicked-up and on their best behavior.

Spook, however, can't suppress his inner clown. Instead of shaking her hand, he says, "Madam, it is a pleasure to meet you. I've heard so much about you." Afterward, he kisses the back of her hand and bows.

Art elbows him.

Spook reacts. "Ouch! You're right, Art. Why are we being so starchy? She's family now." He engulfs her in a bear hug.

Connie, in the midst of the embrace, says with a smile, "Oh my!"

Everyone laughs like old friends.

Hank looks at Connie and hooks his thumb toward Spook who's wearing a goofy grin. "Don't mind him. His head slammed into the backboard one too many times."

After the introductions, it's off to the gym.

Connie sits front row center and is taken in by the college atmosphere. While the cheerleaders haven't performed, they seem professional compared to her girls, even though she thinks the Galileo uniforms are much nicer. She might be slightly biased considering she designed and crafted them. Besides watching Hank, she keeps a close eye on any cheer moves she could borrow.

While basketball is not a popular sport at Stanford, winning creates a buzz, and the freshmen boys become the talk of the campus. Basketball is suddenly hot, and it starts a nearly tangible energy among the crowd. The court, too, is generating its own palpable energy, and while Hank is its center, Connie is the reason—the X factor. Together with John Bunn's command to shoot and Hank's acceptance to do so, Connie's physical presence sets up a perfect trifecta. Hank can barely contain the whirlwind whipping around inside his gut, and by the time the warmups and pep-talk are complete, he stands on the sidelines like a boxer waiting for the bell. When the whistle blows, Hank flies onto the court, takes his position, and waits for the center jump.

Art tips the ball to Hank, and from that moment on Hank is a magician who makes himself vanish in one location and appear seconds later in another. He is rebounding, stealing, dribbling, passing, and to Bunn's delight, shooting. Hank is sinking layups, foul shots, and spectacular running twenty to forty-foot one-handers that enchant the Pavilion. The more he shoots, the louder they clamor for more. The few volunteers assigned to security that evening are unnerved by a crowd on the brink of a riot. Hank is feeding off the crowd and the crowd off Hank, and since he is never winded, Bunn doesn't take him out. In fact, he gets better as the game wears on. Connie is glued to Hank's every move and marvels at his athleticism, grace, and authority. She loves that Hank has control over a thousand people.

Hank scores seventeen points by halftime, thirty-one by the start of the third quarter, and forty-two as the game nears its finale. Hank starts breaking scoring records shortly after the fourth quarter is underway. Dr. Elliot begins the night in his regular seat, buried in the Pavilion crowd, but by the final minutes his excitement drives him onto the court.

Dr. Elliot cheers another Luisetti basket and shouts to Bunn over the chanting crowd, "He's on fire tonight!"

Bunn responds, "If he gets six more points, he'll be the first ever to score fifty in one game, but he's only got fifty-eight seconds to do it!"

Elliot jumps up and shouts, "Shoot, Hank! Shoot!"

The Stanford bench laughs but focus on the court where Dinty steals the ball and passes to Art. He wings it to Howie, who passes to Hank. He shoots and scores.

For the past quarter, every one of the Stanford players is intent on seeing what Hank can do if they keep dishing to him. Every time he passes to someone, the ball comes right back.

At one point, he calls a time out and gathers his team in a huddle. "C'mon guys, you're feeding me too much. We're a team, so let's play the game the way it should be played."

He claps, they clap, and they all jog onto the court.

Hank inbounds the ball and passes it to Spook, who passes it right back. Hank passes it back to Spook, and Spook passes it back again.

Art laughs so hard his ticked defender growls, "What's so funny?"

Hank passes to Dinty who sends it right back again. Hank finds an opening and takes his shot.

With seconds remaining, Hank dribbles low to the ground, snaking through a myriad of players and exploding for his forty-eighth point up near the foul line. He hangs in the air, leaning backward, and releases the ball. It arcs and slides through the net. The Pavilion rafters tremble from the raucous crowd.

The visiting coach calls for a time and screams the order to his team, "Run out the clock! Do not pass and do not shoot! That kid's not making history on my watch!"

They inbound the ball away from Hank, but Dinty intercepts the pass by smacking it toward Hank who's on it in a flash. With three seconds left, he turns, leaps high in the air, and releases a stratospheric jump shot. The buzzer sounds right after he shoots. The whole Pavilion falls silent as the ball seems to sail in slow motion on its historic journey to the hoop. When the ball swishes through, a collective gasp is followed by near pandemonium. Hank, with his arm around Dinty, jogs off the court in triumph as the crowd chants the name of their hero.

* * *

HANK SHOCKS THE fans, the opposing team, and the basketball world. No one has ever accomplished such a feat. Fifty points by one player is unthinkable, unorthodox, and to some, unacceptable. Whether they want to accept it or not, however, stories of Hank's exploits make their way clear across the country.

* * *

AFTER THE GAME, Hank and Connie jog to the Palo Alto train station. When they arrive, Hank looks at his watch and down the tracks. Practicing his habit of filling in the blanks, he breaks the silence by saying, "We made it with a few minutes to spare."

"Oh Hank, I had such fun! This was the most exciting day of my life."

A train is heard in the distance, and he looks in the direction of the sound. "Well… we made it by seconds anyway!"

"Thanks for inviting me, Hank." Connie gives him a kiss on the cheek.

She pulls back, they lock eyes, and their heads bend slowly toward each other. Their lips gently touch, then press together hard. The train screeches in behind them. Wind slaps at their hair and clothes. They pull back slowly and open their eyes again.

A voice is heard in the distance, "All aboard!"

He gives her a quick peck on the lips before she runs onto the train.

Hank rushes up to the doors. "I'll call you later tonight."

"I'll call you," she replies.

Hank says to himself, *I'll be waiting.*

Connie appears at the window, and they wave to each other as the train pulls away.

CHAPTER FOURTEEN

THE DOMINATION OF the Stanford freshmen over the entire league has begun. Connie comes to every game for the rest of the season. She is so much a part of the group, Bunn allows her to travel with them when they are away—not only is she pleasant to be around, but she is, in Bunn's reasoning, his star player's muse. The opposing teams, their coaches, and their fans are fascinated with this new phenom. People travel from miles away to see if he really exists or if he is some kind of myth. Often, the opposing fans can't help but get caught up in the young San Franciscan's celebrity, and they cheer on Hank's heroics. People can't help themselves—they love Hank Luisetti.

* * *

AT THE END of the year, Hank and Dinty stand in front of the wall admiring the newspaper clippings. One clipping sits alone in the center of the last row.

IT'S All OURS! Undefeated Freshmen Win 1935 Conference Title - Luisetti Leads All With 30!

Luisetti Honored at Stanford - His 305 Points Are Most Ever by A Freshman.

A car horn blasts.

Dinty says, "That's my old man. Meet you downstairs."

After Dinty leaves, Hank removes his top dresser drawer and empties it into an open suitcase on his bed. A picture lands face up. It's of a smiling Stefano with his arm around Hank whose legs are encased in the metal braces. Hank holds a bamboo fishing pole with a fish dangling off the end. He looks at it for a beat, puts it in his wallet, grabs his suitcase, and exits the room.

* * *

HANK'S TIME AT home is similar to the Christmas break. Amalia works at the store so she can return home early; however, this time Connie is a constant companion. Hank also spends time at Connie's, and both families are enamored of their newest member — the exception being Stefano. He works extra hours when Hank is home and hears all about Connie from Amalia but never meets her. During the day, Hank earns a few bucks working with Ricky Durán at Galileo, where Ricky coaches a six-week basketball and soccer camp. Hank always keeps an eye out for Miss. Fogarty emerging from a hidden stairwell or scurrying out from a shadow. He wonders if she really does live somewhere in the bowels of Galileo High. Even though the reality is obvious, folklore is much more entertaining.

Hank puts money aside all summer for a surprise date with Connie that will take place just before he returns to Stanford. He picks a day and tells Connie to mark her calendar, but he provides no other details. Connie gets a kick out of how excited he is when he talks about it. She thinks it's cute. Every now and again he reminds her, and she pretends to forget.

"We have a date?" she asks.

A week prior to the big day, Hank tells Connie to wear a

swimsuit. It is to take place on a Monday, but the weather forecast calls for torrential rain. Connie, Ricky, and his nonna mention that, but Hank tells everyone they are wrong.

Hank says with an air of confidence, "Monday is going to be a gorgeous day, the best day of the whole summer." Without pretending or using positive thinking strategies, he believes it without a doubt.

It begins drizzling early Sunday morning, and by Sunday night it is as though Poseidon and Zeus are collaborating on the perfect storm.

"The only person in a boat tomorrow will-a be Noah," Carmela says.

Hank bets her a quarter that it is going to be a sunny day, and he gives Connie a call that night to remind her to wear her swimsuit.

She asks, "Why? Will I be swimming to your house?"

They both laugh.

Connie thinks he is kidding about the swimsuit part, but before they hang up he says, "See you tomorrow morning at seven, and don't forget your swimsuit."

She thinks he's adorable.

Hank calls Ricky to remind him about the car he'd asked to borrow as an added touch. Ricky also thinks he's crazy and suggests an alternate plan, but Hank says he will meet him at the school by 6:40 a.m.

Hank prepares everything he needs for the date before going to bed, and rhythmic raindrops create the soothing background noise for a perfect night's sleep. He closes his eyes at 11:15 p.m. and wakes up at 6:15 a.m. without an alarm. He stretches his way over to the window, pokes open the Venetian blinds, and sunlight pierces his pupils. He stumbles back, rubs his eyes, and smiles. Being blinded by the sun never felt so good. He gathers his belongings and leaves a note on the kitchen table, reminding his grandmother about their bet and the money he will never see. Regardless, he will never let her live it down, which is worth far more than the quarter.

When Hank meets Ricky at 6:40, his friend says, "Maybe you should quit school to become a meteorologist... or fortune teller."

Hank smiles with raised eyebrows and takes the keys. "I'll see you around eight tonight. Okay?"

"You can have it for as long as you like!"

Hank winks, starts the car, and drives away with a grin.

Connie is waiting outside when Hank pulls up in front of her house. She looks like she walked off the cover of a women's magazine. She's wearing a yellow and black cotton sundress, a black, big-rimmed summer hat, and large black sunglasses. No matter how many times he sees her, he is always amazed by her style and unearthly beauty. Hank gets out of the car and walks to Connie, who is smiling and sitting with her legs crossed in an Adirondack chair. When he gets close, she pulls an umbrella out from behind her.

"I don't think you'll be needing that."

"I might need it for the sun."

"Swimsuit?"

"Under here." Connie points to her dress. "You can see it later."

Hank kisses her and the two walk to the car.

"Where are we going?

"It's a surprise!"

They pull up to the docks and onto an awaiting boat near the market at Fisherman's Wharf. Even though Connie has lived in San Francisco her whole life, her father isn't a fisherman, and she's never been on a boat before. Hank makes sure everything will go perfectly. He brings food, drinks, fishing poles, bait, and everything else needed for the day.

The sixteen-foot wooden boat has a V-shaped bow, with a bench across its square stern, and an outboard motor hanging from the transom. Hank, shirtless and wearing black sunglasses, kneels on the bench and steers the boat from the tiller. Connie sits on the port side in her black one-piece bathing suit and holds her hat as Hank skims the boat across the bay. They cruise around for a while before Hank stops at an old fishing spot that he and Stefano frequented when he was a boy. He tosses the anchor and begins baiting the lines.

Connie winces as he hooks a worm. "The poor thing... I'm sure that was painful."

After the job is complete, Hank offers the pole to Connie. "Here you go."

"I don't know, Hank."

"There's nothing to it. I used to do this with my dad when I was a kid."

Hank nestles behind Connie and holds the pole in front of her. "Hold the bottom with your right hand." He wraps his hand over hers. "The left hand's under the reel with your thumb on this leather strip." He puts his hand and thumb on hers and releases the line into the water. "The sinker will hit the bottom, and the moving worms will entice the flounder that lay on the bottom on their sides."

"How can they see the worms if they are on their sides?"

"They have both eyes on the same side of their heads, so they can see what's happening above them. When one bites, put pressure on your thumb. That prevents the fish from running out the line."

"How will I know when he bites it? Ohh! It's biting it. It's biting it!"

The pole arcs and the line zips. Connie screams, and Hank helps her reel in the fish. They pull a large dangling flounder out of the water, then Hank unhooks it and tosses it in a tub.

Connie claps as she speaks, "Let's do that again!"

Hank looks at her with squinted eyes. "I thought you were concerned about the worms."

As luck would have it, Connie hooks fish after fish while Hank catches none. He even throws his line in next to hers, and she still gets one. After her fifteenth catch, Hank says it is time she learns how to unhook it.

He holds the line above the hooked fish and Connie makes an attempt, but when she touches it, it flaps around.

"I can't. You do it. I think it's mad at me."

"I can't say I blame him."

Hank holds the fish while Connie carefully unhooks it and drops it in the tub.

She smells her fingers. "Pee-yew!"

"Did you have fun today?" Hank asks.

Connie nods her head with wide-eyed, childlike enthusiasm.

"Now for the best part."

As the evening sun dwindles away, Hank locates another familiar area between San Francisco and Angel Island, where he and Connie kneel, port side, and feed porpoises.

Connie says, "Oh, they're beautiful! I love this!"

"My father used to bring me here when I was a kid. I wanted to swim with them—be one of 'em."

Connie absorbs Hank with sensual eyes and breathes in deep.

Hank goes on, "They're smart, fast, acrobatic, and free to

roam the open seas. What animal would you be?"

She ponders a moment before saying, "A house cat—a Siamese with blue eyes. I'd snuggle with my family while we listened to the radio, and I'd purr as they pet me."

The two stare at each other and she purrs. Hank smiles and moves close to her and kisses her softly. She looks up at him with tears welling in her eyes.

"What's wrong, Connie?"

"Nothing, silly. I'm just...happy. I love you... I'm so in love with you, Hank."

"I love you too."

They hug.

"This is the best day of my life," she says.

Connie snuggles into Hank's chest. The muscles ripple in his arms as he squeezes her tight, kisses the top of her head, and gently strokes her cheek.

CHAPTER FIFTEEN

A GROUP OF dark-haired, teenage boys play cards around a picnic table in a Brooklyn park. Quarters, dimes, and nickels are piled in the table's center. Thin bottles of Coke, Fresca, and Orange Crush, and bowls of chips and pretzels are strewn about. They talk with thick, New York accents and wear button down shirts and dress slacks. The top button of their shirts is unfastened, and their thin ties are not tight to their necks, but casually loosened on this summer day. They all stand approximately five ten with the exception of Art Hillhouse, a burly six-foot seven monster with mitts that resemble bear paws. He wears an off-white, wide-banded Panama hat and has small teeth for a guy his size. Irving Torgoff wears a thin-banded fedora with a turned-up brim. He's thin with a large nose and a small mouth. Jules Bender, the handsomest of the lot, has dark, wavy hair. He's the only boy with his tie pulled tight to his neck. He wears a wide-rimmed fedora with a high crown and a snapped-down brim that covers half of his eyes. Ben Kramer wears a small, straw fedora with a black band. He has one front tooth that's shorter and darker than the others. Leo Merson wears his fedora tilted back and pats his forehead with a handkerchief. Ken Norton also wears his hat tilted back and moves a toothpick around his mouth.

Six girls with polished nails, modest make-up, and jewelry all wear belted, cotton dresses falling just below the knee. Their short, dark hair is wavy or curled. They gab and drink from soda bottles with straws at a table adjacent to the boys. Swing music plays from a blue 1935 Packard Twelve that's a short distance away, and hamburgers sizzle on a black grill. The grill is tended by Myron Sewitch whose black straw fedora has a little red feather in the band. Danny Kaplowitz is kissing a girl a short distance away from the group under a large sycamore tree.

Irving shouts, "Danny, don't suffocate her."

Danny continues kissing and raises his middle finger.

Hillhouse looks at Jules. "I'll see your fifty cents and raise you fifty." He slides a dollar bill into the pile.

Jules tosses in two coins.

Leo puts down his cards. "Too rich for my blood."

Ben adds, "I'm out."

Kenny drops his cards on the table, face down, saying, "I got nuttin'."

Hillhouse taunts his friends with a sneering smile. "Yous guys shouldn't play if ya can't handle the heat." He shifts his beady eyes toward Jules.

"Beat a king's-high full house, Jules!" Hillhouse slaps his cards down, face up, and cackles from the back of his throat.

Jules looks at the cards, unfazed. He nonchalantly grasps his jaw with his thumb and index finger, slowly drags them down to his chin stubble, and raises his head to the point where his eyes can peek out from under the brim of his hat. He looks at Hillhouse while turning over his hand—an aces-high full house.

Hillhouse slams his fists onto the table making a Coke bottle rocket up. "Shit!"

Leo says, "Why do we even bother?"

Irving smiles. "That's why I folded. I'm no shmendrik."

Hillhouse pounds his bear paws onto the table again knocking over a half-full Coke. "He can't win every time. Shit!"

Irving belly laughs.

In one motion, Hillhouse grabs Irving by the shirt and drags him across the table as if he were weightless. Hillhouse growls at him, saying, "Nobody laughs at me!"

Irving responds with a weak reply. "Hey, watch it, Art."

Everyone, including the two lovers, are around the table in a flash.

Jules, as even keeled as he was when he revealed his hand, says, "Arty what are you doin'? We're all friends here… C'mon now."

Hillhouse spits out, "I hate to lose!"

"That's why we love you, big guy. Now kiss and make up."

Art looks at Jules with a curled lip then bursts out laughing. He lifts Irving off the ground by the shirt and says, "You're lucky I like you!" He releases Irving who drops to the ground.

"Hey Joanie, take a picture of me and da boys, will ya?" Danny says.

Hillhouse bellows, "Irving! C'mere, ya ugly bastard!"

Joanie picks up a large black camera from the table as the boys clump together. Hillhouse wraps his massive arm around Irving in a near headlock, his hairy hand under Irving's chin.

Joanie puts her eye to the camera while rotating the lens right and left. Satisfied with the clarity, she says, "Okay. Everyone say, mazel tov."

They pose and smile. "Mazel tov!"

The camera clicks.

"May this season be as grand," says Myron.

Hillhouse asks, "What the hell does mazel toff mean, anyway?"

MADNESS

* * *

THE DAY AFTER the surprise date, Connie's mother, Rosaria, cleans and fillets the fish and prepares a feast. She dips the flounder in egg and seasoned breadcrumbs and fries them in garlic-flavored olive oil. Each plate has a few fresh lemon wedges from Rosaria's potted lemon trees. The dish is accompanied by broccoli rabe, sautéed in olive oil and garlic, and potato croquettes—one of Rosaria's specialties. Connie ribs Hank by reminding everyone that it is she who is responsible for the bounty; however, Hank deserves some credit because he was the one who baited the hooks. Hank smiles and reminds the family that he also removed the fish once she caught them. The salad, following the main course, is a mixture of lettuce and wild dandelion greens, black olives, and plum tomatoes from Rosaria's garden.

Everything about this day is special, and when Connie says grace, she thanks God for her many blessings, such as the food before them and for the family gathered around the table. She adds, with a big smile, "Especially Daddy who is here with us tonight instead of New York, Chicago, Los Angeles, or Paris."

Hank and Connie make the most of his last days at home and see each other nearly every hour of the day. They go to the beach, picnics, a town fair, and on many long walks.

On the eve of Hank's departure, he and Connie walk hand in hand up to her front door. She puts her arms around his neck, leans her forehead against his, and speaks softly. "The summer went by so fast." She presses her nose to his. "I don't want you to go."

"Me too, but I'm also excited to get back to school and start the new season."

Connie backs up and says with a half-smile, "That wasn't the response I was hoping for."

Hank takes Connie by the shoulders, gently places his forehead against hers, and looks directly into her eyes. She closes her eyes and slowly opens them, unpacking her silky emerald spheres.

He speaks in a whispery tone. "We'll see each other on weekends and every single day between semesters."

She carves out a tight-lipped smile, takes a breath to speak, but pauses for a few beats. "What happens after you graduate?"

Hank rolls his eyes to that upper right region of the forehead, where people often search for thoughts, then casually leans his body against the door, "I'd like to travel a little. Eddie keeps telling me how great it is overseas. Plus, there are a few basketball teams that play in professional tournaments around the country."

Connie swallows hard, looks away, and then back to Hank. "Is there a possibility of you getting a business degree so you could manage your family's businesses?"

"There'd be a better chance of a mermaid crawling out of the San Francisco Bay and ordering a dozen clams at Fisherman's Wharf." He shakes his head. "My father hasn't spoken to me since I left for Stanford."

"Hank… you're his only son, and this thing between you two will end. If you think your mother will allow it to go on forever, you're being naive."

He looks away.

With renewed vigor, Connie says, "It'll work itself out, and think how great it would be if you had a business right in town. Your future would be set!"

Hank flinches, knits his brow, and studies her face as if

he's trying to figure out if it's actually Connie standing before him.

"Why are you looking at me that way?"

"Connie, I…" He pauses to collect his thoughts. "Let's not talk about my father and my future right now. I want to live my life in the present, and at the moment, I'm playing basketball for Stanford University, and I have you, the best girl in San Francisco." He puts his arms around her and gives her a quick kiss.

"Just little old San Francisco?"

"The entire world!"

"That's better." She offers a quick smile.

"I'll call you right after I settle in, and I'll see you on Saturday, right?"

"Of course. I'm coming on Saturday…" Connie's eyes glisten. "I really love you, Hank."

"I love you too."

He places his large hands on her cheeks, his thumbs on either side of her mouth, and kisses her long and deep. He looks in her eyes and smiles. Connie smiles and hugs him tightly. They pull away.

Hank takes a few steps and turns back. "Have sweet dreams."

"You too."

He continues down the path from Connie's home and into the street. He turns again, smiles, and waves. Connie smiles and waves back, and Hank turns and vanishes into the fog. Connie's smile fades. For a few moments, she looks at the silent, hazy space where Hank had been before she turns away, opens the door, and goes inside. The door shuts and a bolt snaps into place.

CHAPTER SIXTEEN

THE NEXT DAY, Hank, Dinty, Spook, Art, and Howie are hanging out in Hank's dorm. Dinty unpacks his clothes from a suitcase on top of his dresser, Art tosses a football to Howie sitting on Hank's bunk, Spook concentrates on the newspaper shrine, and Hank sits at the desk balancing a basketball on each index finger.

Dinty looks at Hank. "You're not going to join the circus with Enrico Rastelli, are you?"

Hank smiles. "No, but my old coach says I should pursue meteorology or fortune telling."

"We all have to pick majors this year," Art says.

Spook, still fixed on the shrine, blurts out, "Hey Dint, you going to take these clippings down from last year or are you going to keep it going?"

"Keeping it going."

Art passes the football. "I don't know about you guys, but I was itching to get back to school. Last year was magical."

Hank looks at him.

Dinty says, "I thought I was the only weirdo who wanted to come back to school."

Howie receives a pass. "Think we could do it again on varsity? The talent has to be up a few notches from last year."

Dinty calls for the ball. "It's more about chemistry than talent, so we'll definitely compete on this level."

"And it's our second year together," adds Art.

Spook is still focused on the wall. "I was so awkward in grade school."

MADNESS

Howie tosses a pillow that crushes the side of Spook's head. "You still are!"

Without missing a beat, Spook says, "I was insignificant until basketball. I didn't have friends. I was a clumsy has-been, and, believe it or not, I hardly ever spoke up—even when kids bothered me. Once I found basketball, I was suddenly popular."

Art and Howie look at each other, bewildered.

"I went from being a dip to a movie star, but nothing beats last year. Jeez, I don't want this to end."

Hank puts down the basketballs. "I agree with everyone, but lately I've been thinking of it as fate—like we were all destined to be at Stanford when Bunn arrived. I've never experienced the feeling I get when I step onto the court with you guys. Something clicks in my brain."

Dinty looks around at the guys and then back at Hank. "We all talked about that last year. You go from being a sweet-heart to a ravenous predator once your foot touches the court floor."

"You were great at Galileo, but you didn't have the edge you have here" Art adds.

"I'm with Spook," Hank says, now fired up. "I don't want this to end, but it will, so let's not waste one second of it. We are going to put Stanford on the map by winning the Pacific Coast League championship this year, next year, and the year after!"

He walks over to Spook and shakes his hand. Without another word, each member of the team shakes hands, swearing a silent oath to both himself and his teammates.

* * *

WHETHER IT IS one specific thing or some combination of talent, chemistry, magic, fate, or commitment, the Stanford Indians, led by a free-wheeling coach and a group of sophomores, hit the league like a wrecking ball, winning their first fifteen consecutive games. Then, one by one, the Indians start going down. During their thirteenth game, Art is hit with a horrendous flu, which sidelines him for two weeks and curtails his usefulness in the weeks that follow. The flu spreads to the Zonne brothers a few days later. When Dinty starts showing symptoms, Bunn secures separate dorms for each of his players, trying to prevent the virus from wiping out his whole team. Dinty's flu turns out to be a cold, but it is a bad strain, and he is out for a week. Like Art, Dinty doesn't regain his health and loses his starting position. Without Art, the Zonne brothers, and Dinty, the Indians are blown out in their sixteenth game by the Golden State Bears. Howie is the next to fall when he receives a season-ending wrist fracture midway through the seventeenth game.

They bounce back in their next one, but game nineteen is John Bunn's worst nightmare. Hank is knocked out cold at the start of a game against UCLA when he and another player smash heads. Hank lay motionless in an ungraceful, facedown position but begins moving by the time John Bunn charges over. He returns to the game but doesn't look right, so Bunn sits him. With the game slipping away, Hank begs to go back in, and Bunn relents. A few minutes after his return, he becomes entangled with two big guys as the trio leap for a rebound. The heel of one of the clunkers lands on Hank's ankle when they hit the floor, and Hank goes down for the second time. This time, he is out for good and unavailable for the next two games.

Although he returns, he hobbles on that taped ankle right

up to the game that decides the Pacific Coast Champions. Hank spends most of the game on the bench, since he reinjured his ankle slightly after the opening tap. The season seems to be over for the Indians by the beginning of the fourth quarter when the Bears are up by fifteen. But Hank convinces Bunn to give him another chance. He goes on a tear and scores thirty points in the fourth quarter, which is just enough to give Stanford the title and its best single-season record with twenty-two wins and seven losses. Dr. Elliot initiates a grand event to honor the team's achievements and publicize Stanford as the new standard in men's college basketball.

The team sits in two rows on the apron of a temporary outdoor stage, erected on the school's majestic quadrangle facing the magnificent Stanford Memorial Church. In the front row, from right to left are Art, Howie, Spook, Dinty, Hank, H.B., Bobby, Phil, John, Nobbs, and John Bunn. Standing center stage at a podium in front of an oblong microphone is Governor Frank Merriam, a balding man in his early seventies, wearing a tailored suit and a glittery smile. Dr. Elliot stands to Merriam's right, and to his left is a large gold trophy proudly displayed on a table draped with a metallic silver and gold covering.

Miles Lee and several other photographers kneel in the center aisle of the packed quad where Connie sits in the front row.

Governor Merriam addresses the crowd. "It is my pleasure to present this prestigious trophy to the 1936 PCC champions, the Stanford Indians."

He slowly hands Dr. Elliot the large, sparkling trophy, assuring that photographers record the moment. Before sitting, Merriam waves to the audience and the cameras with a plastic smile.

Dr. Elliot speaks into the microphone. "Thank you, Governor. We are here tonight, not only to accept this prestigious award but to honor an individual who's added several pages to basketball's history book. This man is a fierce competitor, who scored thirty-two points in thirty-two minutes in the opening game of the conference series. In the finals, he led us to a four-point victory over the Bears by scoring thirty points during the fourth quarter."

Bunn winks at Hank.

Elliot continues, "Yet, it was not only his superior shooting ability, but his all-around play that earned Hank Luisetti both the College Player of the Year Award and the unanimous choice as All-American forward."

The crowd applauds Hank as he stands and walks to the podium. Elliot shakes his hand, then lowers two gold medals over Hank's head as a standing ovation ripples through the audience. Hank humbly smiles and waves to the crowd. Connie stands and claps, but her eyes and mind are preoccupied.

* * *

THE NEXT NIGHT, Stefano enters the kitchen from the back entrance of the Luisetti home. He flicks on the light and places his keys on a hook under the cabinets. He takes off his cap and hangs it on a post at the back of a kitchen chair. While unbuttoning his jacket, he notices his son's face on the cover of a strategically placed newspaper: "Local Boy Wins All-American Forward and College Player of The Year Awards."

Stefano grabs the paper with both hands, holds it close to his face, and carefully places it on the table. He pauses and walks, trancelike, to the light switch and eases it closed with a slow brush of his hand. He slides into a kitchen chair and clamps his hand onto his face; his flattened nose labors for air between his clenched fingers. He releases his grip and stares at nothing in the thorny silence of the room. The whites of Stefano's reddened eyes grow larger at the bottom as he settles on a spot beyond the focus of the kitchen ceiling.

* * *

IN A LOCKER room in Madison Square Garden, Art Hillhouse heaves a newspaper into a cement-block wall with a pop. Leo, Jules, Benny, Danny, Myron, Irving, and Kenny are gathered around. Only Jules is in uniform.

Hillhouse kicks the air. "That's bullshit!"

"It's a damned crime," exclaims Irving.

Benny wags his finger. "They should pick the best player from the best team." He looks around for approval. "Am I right or am I right?"

The boys nod.

Myron throws in. "It's that putz from California who scored the fifty points in one game."

Jules, calm but with the hint of a curled lip, says, "I knew it!"

Hillhouse slams an open locker door against another and takes off his shirt. "What's the big deal about scoring fifty points in some bullshit league? When the mighty West Coast champion Golden State Bears came to the Garden, we humiliated them. They're a joke."

Claire Bee's stealthy entrance goes unnoticed until he speaks, and his passive-aggressive overtones go undetected. "Not dressed yet? Have you forgotten what time the charity match begins this afternoon?"

Hillhouse, in a swiss-cheesed white tank-top, turns with a jerk, plucks the bludgeoned paper from the floor, and thrusts it toward Bee. "Did you see this, Coach?"

Bee's eyes remain fixed on his Herculean center's flexed physique.

"Jules should have won those awards!"

Danny says what everyone else is thinking but wouldn't dare say, "If you cut Jules loose and let him shoot, he'd break every record there is."

Bee was relieved that someone finally said it.

His eyes glide from Danny to the emboldened team clustered before him. Clair begins his address with the placid tones of a therapist. "If one player on a team is looked upon as the star, it becomes an infection. You no longer rely upon each other; instead, you rely upon the star. The rest of the team doesn't feel quite as responsible for production and stop thinking on their own." His pitch rises, his tone slightly sharper. "Arrogance emerges, jealousies and blame follow, and dysfunction becomes a disgruntled bench player—always present, always there—poisoning the air with sidebar conversations that pit player against player."

Clair rubs the stress from his chin, then smacks his open palm into a locker and advances toward the group with a slap of his foot on the cement floor. The veins ripple in his neck each time he stabs the air with a pointed finger. "If that coach from Stanford University wants to make a mockery of this sport that's his business, but that's not the way it will ever be done here! You are the LIU Blackbirds, heralded as the greatest basketball team of all time. You've achieved that distinction as a team." He spits venom. "As a team!" The word team bangs off thick cement and hollow metal. He straightens his tie and flattens his jacket before finishing off with a dose of disappointment and disgust. "Now stop whining, get changed, and act like the champions you are."

The boys, with the collective look of a dog who's torn up a couch pillow, begin unpacking their uniforms and opening lockers.

"I'll expect you upstairs ready for warmups in four minutes." Bee exits the room.

Jules sits on a bench and turns his head in the direction of the departed coach, more with his eyes than with his head. Like a single pulse of a heartbeat, he flashes a menacing scowl at his coach's back, but he buries it before turning toward his teammates. He claps enthusiastically. "C'mon boys. Let's not keep him waiting."

* * *

IN AN UPPER tier of Madison Square Garden, Ned Irish studies a newspaper with the smiling photo of Hank proudly displaying two medals, one in each hand. Footsteps are heard clapping along the maple floor below as Clair Bee appears on the court.

CHAPTER SEVENTEEN

CONNIE VISITS HANK at least once a week and works at the pharmacy Monday through Friday. This doesn't leave time for much else, so she decides to resign her position as Galileo's cheer coach. On Saturday mornings, she normally catches a seven o'clock train to Stanford and arrives home that evening. Overnights are not an option. People of today might wonder why, since coed sleepovers are commonplace these days. Back in the 1930s, however, a young lady's reputation would be ruined if she were to have an overnight with a man if they weren't married. This societal and religious expectation was accepted the same way people accepted writing letters before the advent of computers. One couldn't miss what didn't exist.

Hank usually accompanies Connie back on Saturday nights, sleeps at home, and spends Sunday at Connie's house doing homework and socializing with her family. He takes the nine o'clock train back to Stanford on Sunday night.

After winning the Pacific Coast Conference, receiving two prestigious awards, setting another scoring record, and becoming an on-campus celebrity, Hank is the happiest he's ever been, and basketball is only part of it. With a 3.4 GPA, Hank is excelling academically as well.

Upon completing his second year, he is required to declare a major, and he seeks advice from Stanford's guidance department. Before college, Hank always thought he'd work at the restaurant. Even though Stefano didn't sell Angelo's to Dante as he threatened, Hank doesn't consider that as a possible career choice.

Following a lengthy discussion, Dr. Thames, a portly man with a gray beard who smokes a pipe, suggests an anthropology degree with the possibility of joining the armed forces to become a pilot. Hank hadn't considered joining the military before—that's Eddie's gig. Besides, he isn't sure what anthropology is.

Thames reclines in his chair. "You've expressed a strong desire to travel the world, and you can do that with either of these careers. As an anthropologist, you will explore exotic cultures and peoples."

Isn't it people? Hank thinks.

Thames continues, "If you enter the military with a college degree, you can become an officer and train as a pilot. As an athlete, your quick reflexes would be a considerable asset. You can either choose a career in the military or become a pilot for a private company. I fancy there's a bright future in air travel, Mr. Luisetti."

Hank is intrigued by both choices, so he decides to get an anthropology degree and then enlist in the military to become a pilot.

While getting dressed for a frat party, he interviews himself in front of the mirror in his room. He grips his hair brush and says, "Mr. Luisetti, now that you've won the Pacific Coach Championship and All-American forward three years running, what are your future plans?" Hank answers himself, "I will play in a few basketball tournaments and then enlist in the military to become a pilot."

Dinty and Spook open the door and see Hank standing in his boxer shorts in front of the mirror.

"What are you doing? You crazy man, you!" Spook says.

Hank brushes his hair. "What? I'm getting ready."

Spook smiles. "Did we catch you singing?" He turns to Dinty. "I believe he was singing?"

"C'mon, Hank. We're already ten minutes late," Dinty exclaims.

"Maybe Woody Guthrie over there will sing a few ballads for us tonight," says Spook.

For a few weeks, Hank is known as Woody, a popular balladeer of the times, but the moniker didn't stick.

* * *

THE FINAL SATURDAY, before school ends, Hank, Connie, the rest of the team, and a few girls spend the day at a park not far from the campus. They eat, drink, and play badminton, and the boys toss around a football. While Connie is pleasant, she's not herself — at least the self she's always been. Over the past month, she's distant and Hank doesn't know why, especially since she has been consistently upbeat since her days at Galileo. Hank figures she is tired of train stations and rushing around; however, summer is approaching and it will all work itself out. Hank plans on a few boat excursions this season since Connie loved the last one so much.

Cloud cover and then rain break up the picnic in the early evening. When everyone decides to go to a movie, Connie says she isn't feeling well and asks to get the next train back home. Art drops Hank and Connie at the station, and the two make their way to a damp bench. Connie stares blankly in the direction of the tracks without uttering a word. Hank attempts conversation, but all he receives are one-word responses. He asks her if she likes Howie's new girlfriend, and she doesn't respond at first.

After a few seconds, she asks, "I'm sorry, what did you

say?" Connie's large eyes find her feet, her hands, the tracks, a billboard, or the air in front of her—anywhere but Hank.

"What's the matter?"

Connie answers the train tracks, "I'm tired."

"I know it's been hectic, but this'll be the last train station we see for months. We have the whole summer to look forward to."

Connie doesn't answer right away. When she does, she looks at Hank with a sad smile. "I can see why you look forward to it. You have a girlfriend all summer, and you head back to school in a few months. Then you'll graduate in a few years and be off to who knows where."

Hank tries to respond, but nothing comes out.

Connie speaks to the tracks again. "I can't do this anymore." She shifts her eyes to Hank. "You never talk about a future that includes me."

"I always include you."

"You include me in your everyday life but not in your future, and I can't wait any more. Do you know how much it hurts to ask you to include me? It's pathetic that I have to ask you that."

"I don't understand."

"I think you do. You go to college, play basketball, and have a convenient girlfriend."

Hank's brow wrinkles. "Is that what you think?"

Connie raises her voice, "What am I supposed to think when the only future you talk about involves basketball and some fantasy of traveling the world. Where am I in all of this... or am I in it at all?"

Connie awaits a response, but Hank is shut down once again by truth; he manages only to stutter. "I..." Then his face becomes flushed. He knows what she's going to ask before the words come out.

"What exactly are your plans Hank? I heard Dinty say he had to choose his major by the end of the semester. What did you choose?"

He blurts out, "Anthropology."

Connie winces. "Anthropology? There's a customer at the pharmacy who's an anthropologist. He just got back from South America where he lived with an indigenous tribe for six months."

Hank shoots back, "That's just the major I chose. I really intend on joining the army to become an officer and a pilot."

"The army? The army? When did you decide that?"

"Recently. I was going to tell you."

Connie gets up from the bench and walks slowly toward the tracks, digesting words and fear. She advances toward Hank who's now standing. She sits and he does the same.

She takes his hands, leans in close, and speaks softly, "All I ever wanted from the time I was a little girl was to get married to the love of my life, have babies, and live out my days in San Francisco. I want to live within walking distance of my sisters, my parents, and my nonna. That's my dream... but that dream is dead if you're not in it because I love you, Hank."

He rubs his eyes with his thumbs and lets his hands fall onto his knees. A knot of tension balls up in his stomach. "I can't believe what's happening right now. All this because of my career choices?"

"Your choices sound like you're running away from something." She pauses briefly and straightens her posture. "I need you to commit to a future that includes me, and that should include some of what I want. I'll commit to you right now for the rest of my life, Hank, but I want to hear you say that I'm your future."

Like a referee, the faint sound of a train whistle curtails talk and commands action, yet Hank is frozen.

Connie's face crumples. "I've loved you since high school." Her eyes well up like giant emerald pools, her nose runs, and the dam behind her beautiful eyes bursts.

The train violently roars into the station, screeches to a halt, and opens its doors.

Connie looks at Hank's blank stare, gets up, and runs to the train.

He stands, moves forward, and stops. The doors slam shut.

He sees her sitting with her hands cupped over her face, her shoulders rocking from violent sobs.

In a trancelike state, he stands alone on the empty platform, staring in the direction of the train long after it vanishes.

Rain pelts the ground around the platform as wisps of Connie's sweet pheromones swirl in the air around him.

* * *

"HIS NAME IS Ned Irish," says John Bunn to Dr. Elliot.

The doctor sips tea while the men sit across from each other in Elliot's office.

"He's invited us to tussle with LIU next season—on December 30 at Madison Square Garden," Bunn adds.

Dr. Elliot grasps the teacup ear with his index finger and thumb. His outstretched pinky points upward as he takes a quick sip and places the dainty porcelain cup on its saucer. "The publicity in New York would be most beneficial. When did he call?"

"Three weeks ago."

Elliot's eyes widen.

"I'd have told ya sooner, but I wanted to make a few calls."

"Why's that?"

Bunn rubs his chin as he talks. "LIU pounded the Bears last year after they won the Pacific Coast Championship. Also, LIU is riding a thirty-eight-game winning streak, a national record. They set that record in what's considered the toughest division in college basketball. However, it's not only those factors that concern me. It's the conditions."

"Conditions?"

Bunn shrugs. "At the early part of our season we'd have to take a train across the country and play these guys on their home turf, right in the heart of New York City."

Elliot ponders this for a few moments. "Are you saying we can't win?"

"Not saying that, but... I just want you to know what we're up against."

Elliot takes a sip of tea and returns it to the saucer with a clink. "I understand, but you know we must accept."

Bunn pushes out a breath, pauses, and says, "I'm not sure if we're ready for 'em just yet. If we lose, it'll set us back."

Dr. Elliot slurps the last of his tea and smiles. "Then don't lose, Mr. Bunn."

CHAPTER EIGHTEEN

HANK RESUMES HIS summer job with Ricky Durán at Galileo, where organizing sports equipment is the first task of the year. Hank sits on the gym floor near a few canvas bags. Amidst basketballs, soccer balls, and baseball equipment, he balances three basketballs on top of his outstretched palm. Ricky stands a few feet from Hank writing notes on a clipboard. When he finishes, he tucks the pencil in its holder above the chrome clip and studies Hank for a few seconds.

"That's amazing, Angelo! Where'd you learn that?"

Hank doesn't answer right away; instead, he releases the balls and looks at Ricky flatly. "Taught myself."

Concern tilts Ricky's head before he walks over. "Are you okay?"

Hank points to the equipment mess. "I'm fine. We bagging this?"

"First we have to look it over to see what's good, what can be repaired, and what goes in the garbage."

"I looked though it already and threw a few things out. This stuff's all good."

Hank grabs a canvas bag and puts basketballs into it. Ricky takes a different bag and starts with the soccer balls.

Hank's rapid movements are fueled by nervous energy. "We broke up."

Ricky continues working. "I see. I'm very sorry to hear that, Angelo."

Hank starts on the baseball bag. "Out of the blue, she wants to plan my future—commit to marriage."

Ricky holds the bag so Hank could load it easier. "Angelo, nothing as big as that comes out of the blue. You've just been missing the signs. Women want men who are grounded, someone who will love them and provide their babies with a stable home."

Hank zips the cord of the bag closed. "Are we putting these in the closet?"

"We are."

They each grab a sack and walk to an open closet a few feet away.

Hank looks down. "If I think about it, I lose my mind. So I push it out of my head."

Ricky places a bag in the storeroom. "That may be what feels best right now, but things like this have a way of resurfacing. Listen to your gut, Hank. It sounds like it's telling you something."

Hank hands him a bag. "I'll be all right."

Ricky plops another bag in the closet and pats Hank on the back as they walk onto the gym floor.

* * *

THE SUMMER PASSES slowly. Ricky keeps Hank busy five days a week from seven in the morning until three in the afternoon, but the hours that follow are more of a challenge. After three, the real work begins. Often, he will try to keep his mentor after work by talking to him about everything, except Connie. His first hurdle is bridging the gap between Ricky and his mother who arrives home at 6:30 p.m. He looks forward to making dinner with her and playing cards.

Amalia tries to talk about Connie on a few occasions, but Hank shuts it down. It hurts Amalia to see her son suffering, and if she can't help him by talking, she does what any mother would do—she feeds him. She makes all of his favorite foods, even her famous twist cookies, a Luisetti family recipe only baked during Christmas. She makes them every week along with ricotta cheesecake and homemade breads, pasta, and focaccia pizza. Her eggplant parmesan is to die for, and one of her secrets is her knack for choosing the perfect eggplant. She picks male eggplants because they have fewer seeds. They have to be long and thin as well.

Amalia cooks and Hank eats. He turns those meals into an extra ten pounds of solid muscle. When thoughts of Connie arise, he forces them out of his head with basketball. Sometimes he stays at the gym after Ricky leaves for the day, and other days he plays at the park. Hank works on two areas of his game: shooting and dribbling. He shoots the ball from every corner of the court and parks himself at the foul line for hours with a canvas bag full of balls. He becomes so proficient, he begins shooting with his eyes closed. Hank creates obstacle courses and dribbles through them, again and again, until he nearly passes out from fatigue. He also dribbles down Russian Hill to the park and then back up again, building strong leg and core muscles.

While Hank does his best to fight painful thoughts during the day, no mental strategies can tame the night. He constantly dreams of Connie and wakes up sweating and gasping for air as though his lungs forget how to breathe while he sleeps. He wheezes as one might in the throes of an asthma attack. Some of his dreams aren't even about Connie. These are scary manifestations of distress, faceless terrors, or cars without brakes that crash into trees, walls, or other cars. Some careen off cliffs or bridges.

Contrary to every other year in his life, summer becomes

a race to the new school year. It is a difficult race, but Hank is thrilled when he crosses the finish line and walks into his dorm where his four brothers wait for him.

* * *

IN A BACKROOM of Ian's Steakhouse in Manhattan, Nat Holman, Howard Cann, and Buck Freeman share a round table with Clair Bee who is in the midst of a speech. He stands below a moose head mounted above a stone fireplace. Another ten tables are filled with basketball dignitaries and other special guests. Several news reporters are moving about, snapping photos and scribbling on note pads.

Clair Bee clasps his hands together in a folded prayer formation and uses it as a gavel in the air to accentuate his words. "The emphasis is on defense, not the other way around." He spreads his hands out near his shoulders and looks as though he's holding a basketball in each palm, once again gaveling the air for affect. "Altering this basic fundamental changes the game dramatically. Besides, employing that rule will exhaust these kids. The action will never stop!"

A reporter with a white carnation pinned to red suspenders states, "Some say eliminating the center jump after each basket will induce higher scoring and create more excitement like on the West Coast."

Nat Holman stands. "Those people don't know the difference between their ass and their elbow." He sits and stands again. "And you can quote me on that, Bill!" He laughs at his own joke.

Clair Bee, upstaged by Holman, shakes his head and sits. Ned Irish and his associate, Brian Hurley, a man in his thirties who dresses like Ned, enter. Ned sits next to Clair Bee, and

Hurley sits to Ned's right.

As soon as Irish sits, Clair leans into his ear. "Do you believe this, Ned? I know it's only a one-year trial, but I never thought something like this could happen... not in New York!"

"I'm only a promoter, Clair." Irish clinks his glass a few times.

Once he has the room's attention, he stands. "Good evening, Gentlemen. We're here tonight to celebrate the start of the 1936-37 basketball season, and while everyone should be jubilant, there's tension over the legislation regarding a one-year trial to determine if the West Coast's concept of eliminating the center jump after each basket is in the best interest of the game. I can't change the rules, but what I have done is provide you with a stage to let your voices be heard."

Coaches listen, reporters scribble, while others snap photos.

"I've arranged a game at the Garden between LIU and the Pacific Coast Champion Stanford Indians. Their coach, John Bunn, has become the face of change in college basketball. The game will be the featured event of a holiday doubleheader. The first game will be a rematch between NYU and Georgetown."

Flashbulbs pop and men chatter among themselves. Irish sits.

A reporter asks, "Any comments, Clair?"

"Defeating Stanford will prove a point."

"What makes you so sure of victory? Stanford racks up a lot of points."

"Good defense will beat good offense every time. And we'll prove that, decisively!"

Brian Hurley leans toward Irish and whispers, "Can you

smell the money?"

* * *

THE LIU/STANFORD MATCH is the main topic of discussion at the first meeting for both LIU and Stanford. For Clair Bee, it isn't a simple east versus west publicity stunt. He has an opportunity to skewer John Bunn and annihilate his brand of basketball. Ned Irish chose LIU to play the Indians, and Clair does not take it lightly. He believes he is personally responsible for basketball's integrity. This will be the most important game of his life. His team, on the other hand, has a score to settle with Luisetti, who, in their opinion, stole Jules' awards.

Stanford sees the game as fun because it involves a cross-country trip. LIU sees it as war, and the Indians have no way to foresee the firestorm that awaits them in Manhattan. The venue is another factor to which the young westerners will not be accustomed. The Stanford Pavilion holds a meager 1,436 people, but Madison Square Garden with all its grandeur holds nearly 18,000 of the most tenacious fans imaginable. They are like a sixth player on the court as their relentless chants and volume have the reputation of unnerving visiting teams. The New York media machine is yet another foreign factor. Stanford is used to Miles Lee and the Stanford Daily, but New York has the New York Times, the Daily News, the New York Post, and several other major publications that will place this east/west showdown on the national stage.

Sitting in classrooms at different ends of the country, the two coaches gather their teams around them to discuss the big game. Each has his own philosophy and expectations.

Clair Bee stands in a classroom facing Benny, Irving, Hillhouse, Jules, Leo, Danny, Kenny, Myron, and newcomers Morty Levine and Elie Gold. The coach, dressed in a jacket and tie, addresses his team with urgency and zeal. "Winning is not enough. We must beat them badly. This is no ordinary game."

At Stanford, John Bunn faces a cheering group including Hank, Art, Dinty, Howie, Spook, Phil, H.B., Bobby, Nobbs, and a transfer student named Sparky Robertson, a long, lanky sophomore from Los Angeles. "It's an ordinary game, only it's some three thousand miles away."

Bee says, "They're an overrated team in an inferior league."

Bunn says, "They're a great team, but you're the best I've ever seen."

Bee says, "You're the best there ever was, but there's a lot on the line, so be prepared for extra practices—tough practices. During the holiday recess, you will not be with your families getting flabby from overeating. We'll be at Grossinger's in the Catskills where we'll remain until game day. You'll be at your best when you step onto that court."

Clair Bee makes a vow to himself that he will bring his team to their peak. However good they were in the past, they will be better this year.

At Stanford, John Bunn ends the meeting by laying out the grueling schedule. "We land in Philly on the twenty-fourth to play Temple, one of the best teams in the East. Playing the Owls gives us a chance to see a respected eastern-division team before stepping into the ring with the Blackbirds. On the twenty-sixth, we'll scrimmage the Georgetown Hoyas in D.C., who'll play at the Garden against NYU the night we play LIU. We'll practice at the Washington facility for the next few days and discuss tactics, match ups, etc. before we dance with them in the big show. We'll take a pass by the Garden on the thirtieth to walk around the place, but I want you away from the commotion. We'll get loose in the lockers beforehand and warmup on the court just before the game."

Spook raises a finger in the air. "Sir, have you scheduled any time for us to meet girls?"

The boys laugh.

Spook looks around with his mouth agape. "What? That's a valid question."

After the meeting, Hank uses John Bunn's office to call the person he is most excited to tell.

Ricky Durán speaks into the phone, "New York, huh? December 30th? My in-laws will be in from Seattle."

"Oh, I didn't expect you to come. I just wanted to tell you about it and thank you for all you've done for me. I wouldn't be doing this if it weren't for you, Mr. Durán."

"I'd love to see you play on the big stage."

Hank smiles. "I'll make you proud, Coach."

Ricky Durán chokes up a little. "Knock 'em dead, Angelo." He places the phone back onto the receiver, wipes a lone tear, and ponders.

CHAPTER NINETEEN

IN A PRACTICE session at the Brooklyn College of Pharmacy gym, Leo covers a sweat-dampened Myron, dribbling with verve.

Clair shadows them, cranking out orders. "Don't let him breathe, Leo! That's it!"

Following Myron and Leo are Benny, dribbling, and Irving, guarding. Moving alongside them is Ira Schwartz, a tall, red-faced man in his forties.

Ira yells, "That's it! Stick to him, Irv!"

Benny and Irving are followed by Kenny, dribbling, and Danny, guarding. Abe Tanenbaum, a man in his fifties with big lips, sprays spit on Danny as he cries, "Press, Danny. Press!"

Danny wipes his face. "If I press any more, I'll foul him." He wipes his hands on his shorts.

"So foul him, only don't let the ref see it!"

Hillhouse is on the opposite side of the court fielding rebounds and passing back to shooters. Jules stands on the foul line, Morty Levine is in the right corner, and Elie Gold is in the left. They rotate positions clockwise after they shoot. Hillhouse passes to Jules who shoots then rotates. Hillhouse rebounds and flings it to Morty who shoots and rotates. They work with assembly line precision.

* * *

CARMELA IS KNITTING at the Luisetti's dining room table.

131

Amalia is standing near Ricky Durán who is holding his hat with both hands.

Amalia touches Ricky's arm. "Sit down. Have-a some demitasse."

"I'd love some, but my dog is tied up outside. Angelo told me about the trip."

Amalia smiles and nods her head. "We so proud of-a him."

"I'm rounding-up some of his old friends for a surprise trip to New York. Your family is welcome to join us."

"That's-a so nice, David. I talk to Stefano when he comes home."

"Great. Here's my number." He removes a piece of paper from his pocket and gives it to Amalia.

She takes the paper and says, "Let me get-a you something to eat. Sit down. Stefano is-a come home soon."

Lady barks outside.

"No thank you, Mrs. Luisetti. I have to go." He looks at Carmela. "Goodbye."

"Buona sera... buona sera," she says without looking.

Amalia follows Ricky to the door and looks at him with reverence. "I wanna thank-a you so much for everything you do for my Angelo. I appreciate."

"No need to thank me. He's a great kid. Good night, Mrs. Luisetti."

"Good-a night, David."

* * *

SITTING ON THE edge of his bed with his elbows on his knees, Hank rubs his forehead with the palms of his hands.

Dinty stands over him. "Just call her, Hank!"

Hank sucks in a breath and blows it out forcefully.

"You care about her, don't you?"

Hank looks at Dinty. "You know I do."

"So call her!"

Hank stands and starts pacing. "You wouldn't understand."

Dinty grabs a chair, spins it around, and sits on it backward with the backrest against his chest. "Hank, you're my buddy and all, but you keep everything locked up inside. I can't help if you don't trust me."

Hank stops pacing, glances at the floor for a beat, and then sits on the bed across from Dinty. He tries to talk but stops. He takes another deep breath and says, "I don't know if you could understand why I let her go because I'm not totally sure either. All I had to do was say a few words, and I could have fixed it. She was looking at me with tears in her eyes, and I stood there like a fool. I can't stop thinking about her eyes looking at me that night. I stood on that platform for three hours after she left. It sounds dumb, but I think it has something to do with my father mapping out my future for me since the day I was born. Look how that turned out. Connie wanted to do that too."

Dinty puts his hand on Hank's shoulder. "I don't think she wants to plan your life, buddy. She just wants to know you love her."

Hank responds with watery eyes, "People tell you they love you. Then stuff happens, and love goes out the window." He sniffles back tears in one huge breath and regains control.

"Hank, I don't believe that for one minute. If someone loves you, they love you. If you want to be with her, go see her. Go tonight. If you wait too long, she'll move on."

Hank nods his head. "You're right."

* * *

ALONE ON THE Stanford Pavilion court at around midnight, Hank wrestles with his demons. He dribbles between his legs and around his back, driving forward, backing up, driving forward again, moving left, pivoting right, and corkscrewing himself around the court with frenetic energy. He leaps, turns in the air, shoots, and rushes the basket before the ball swishes in. He retrieves the ball after a bounce, jumps as high as the rim, and dunks it. He dribbles to the right side, spins, and nails one without looking at the basket. He shoots with his right hand, with his left, and from positions all around the court. All he has to do is get the ball near the basket and it's yanked through the hoop like metal to a magnet. He's on fire.

* * *

WHILE HANK IS using basketball to settle a battle in his mind, the Blackbirds are drubbing their opponents in the opening game of the 1936-37 season three thousand miles away. A leaping Art Hillhouse taps the ball to Jules. Amid a web of arms and legs, the ball is smoothly flicked from Jules to Benny before being passed to Hillhouse, Leo, Irving, and, finally back to Jules, who shoots. The ball ricochets in the rim like a pinball between bumpers and hisses through. The Garden, over 14,000 strong, roars.

The following night, Stanford plays their opening game in front of a sold-out crowd at the Pavilion. Spook dribbles, attempts a reverse move, and his feet get tangled up. Before hitting the floor, he tosses the ball to Hank who uses Spook as a shield. He shoots, scores, and falls over laughing.

MADNESS

Dinty jogs by. "Great move, Spook!"

Spook stands and bows. "I planned that."

The Indians laugh themselves through their first victory of the season. Hank leads all scorers with thirty-two.

* * *

THE BLACKBIRDS CONTINUE their dominance during the second game of the season, where they are squashing the Hampton Pirates—this time at the Hippodrome arena in Manhattan, their alternate venue. Irving Torgoff stands at the foul line for a free throw. He holds the ball with his thumbs on top and fingers pointed toward the floor. He crouches, lowers the ball to his ankles, and spins it underhand using the backboard to score. Flashbulbs pop and the crowd cheers.

Clair Bee claps. "That's it, Irv."

After the field goal, LIU applies man-to-man pressure as Hampton takes out the ball. Jules steals it and steps into a silky layup. Hillhouse pumps his fist. Myron grabs Jules by the shoulders and shakes him as the fans get louder.

* * *

A DIFFERENT TYPE of battle is raging across the country at the Luisetti household.

Amalia, shaking her hand at the wrist with her thumb joined to her fingers, says, "And-a why not?"

"You expect-a me to go away for one week in-a holiday time. Who's-a gonna watch the business?" Stefano asks.

Amalia answers, "Dante!"

"And who's-a gonna watch Dante?"

135

CHAPTER TWENTY

A PASSENGER TRAIN speeding through a quiet night transports the Stanford Indians to the first leg of their cross-country journey. With the exception of the Zonne brothers and Sparky, this is the first time any of the boys have ever been out of San Francisco, and they can hardly wait to step foot on the famed asphalt of the Big Apple.

The team is quartered in an eight-compartment sleeper car with four bunks on each side and a ladder at each end. Black curtains, flowing from the ceiling to the floor, cover the bunks. The east end of the room has a metal pitcher on top of a cabinet. It's covered on all sides by wooden slats to keep it from sliding. Paper cups in the form of a cone are held in a vertical dispenser.

On the right side of the aisle, Hank and Dinty sit in the upper left compartment. Next to them in the upper right compartment is Spook, and Phil and Bobby Zonne are in the lower left. The curtains are closed on the lower right bunk where Art is sleeping. On the left side of the aisle, Nobbs is in the upper right with H.B in the upper left, Sparky in the lower right, and Howie in the lower left compartment. The boys are sitting on the edge of the beds with their legs dangling in the aisle. They are laughing at Spook who has his head stuck through the slit in the curtains.

Art, lower right, rips open his curtains. "Knock it off, Spook. I'm tired!" He closes his curtains in a huff.

The boys laugh louder.

Spook twirls his head from the top of the curtain to the

bottom, contorting his face on the way down. "I'm falling! Ahh!"

Art pulls open his curtains and sticks his head out and up. His and Spook's faces are inches apart. "Cut it out, Jack!"

"Dang, Art. We could use your breath on defense."

Spook sticks his arm through the split in the curtains above his head, grabs his own hair, and pulls his head backward through the curtains.

The boys howl in response.

"You're all nuts!" Art says, going into his bunk and whipping the curtains closed.

Dinty looks at Hank. "Did you call her?"

He shakes his head.

Dinty's focus is diverted when Spook pops from behind his curtains, races down the ladder, runs over to the desk, grabs the pitcher of water, opens Art's curtains, and chucks in the contents. Art yelps, and Spook runs up the ladder and dives into his bunk.

Art comes out, face and hair soaked, holding a shoe. He runs up the ladder, opens Spook's curtains, and fires.

"Ouch! Shoot! That clipped the nose, Art!" Spook opens his curtains and hurls a pillow at Art and a pillow fight ensues.

Dinty jumps down and grabs a pillow off the floor.

Hank sits pensively, then disappears into his bunk and closes the curtains. Spook sees Hank and winds up to toss in a pillow, but Dinty holds his arm and shakes his head. Spook understands not to bother him, then smacks Dinty in the head with the pillow instead.

* * *

AT THE HIPPODROME, Liu is wrapping up a dismantling of the Wesleyan Rams. A tall Ram is about to shoot, and a grimacing Art Hillhouse smacks the ball into the floor. Irving grabs the loose ball and dribbles toward the hoop. He passes to Danny, who passes to Myron. The ball goes to Jules, to Art, and back to Myron who shoots and scores. The buzzer blares, and Hillhouse jumps high in the air smacking his chest with his fist. He leaps up again, grabs the back of the hoop, and does one-armed pull-ups, roaring after each one. The crowd eats it up. Clair Bee watches his boys with delight.

* * *

THE STANFORD TEAM'S four-day train ride ends in Philadelphia on December 24, 1936, at one in the afternoon. Another hour or so, and the whole team would have thrown Spook out the window. Even John Bunn threatens to leave him in Iowa. If Spook isn't giving someone a hot foot or pouring water on anyone's head who happens to walk past his bunk, he is locking people in the bathroom, often after he just finishes using it. His hijinks, however, are easily forgiven. He manages to keep everyone from going stir crazy while being confined to a box for four days. When the Indians pull into the West Philadelphia Railroad Station, they are amped and ready to rock.

They experience their first taste of the eastern-media machine the instant they step off the train. Waiting for them are Eric Parks, a thin man in his thirties with a camera around his neck, and Pat Bradford, a fleshy man in his late twenties, wearing a bowler and holding a picture of John Bunn. The two men comb through passengers discharging from the train.

"That's them!" Parks says.

Bradford does a double take. "Jeez! Look at the size of those guys."

A six-hour delay in Chicago throws off John Bunn's carefully-planned schedule, and he is tense, tired, and a little salty. He worries that the team won't have enough time to mentally prepare for the game, and a loss might affect their psyche. His first order of business is to call Dr. Elliot who asked Bunn, repeatedly, for frequent updates.

Parks and Bradford approach Bunn just as he enters a phone booth.

Bradford, with a pencil in hand, greets Bunn. "Hello, Mr. Bunn. We're from the Philadelphia Tribune. I'm Eric Parks and this is Pat—"

Bunn waves him away "Another time, boys."

Bunn enters the booth and closes the squeaking folding door. The reporters turn their attention to the team.

Parks looks up at the giants. "How do you guys feel about the game against Temple?"

"We can't wait," Art says.

"What's your name, son?" asks Bradford.

"Art Stoefen."

Parks snaps a picture of Art. "You're the younger brother of tennis pro Lester Stoefen, right?"

Art nods proudly.

Howie laughs and pulls Hank aside. "These guys look like Laurel and Hardy."

They both cackle.

"Who's Hank Luisetti?" Bradford asks.

Spook steps in front of Hank, still laughing. "I am, sir!"

"I'll need a picture of you too." Parks snaps a picture of Spook who poses with a talk-show-host smile.

Howie masks his laughter by coughing through it.

Bunn opens the cranky door, steps out, and says, "Mr. El-liot and his wife have the flu so they will not be joining us." John Bunn starts jogging, and the team follows suit with Parks and Bradford in tow.

Bradford asks Hank, "Who's Elliot?"

"Stanford's president. By the way, I'm Hank Luisetti."

The team bursts out laughing.

Hank offers an apologetic look. "We're a little punchy."

Parks winces. "Pranksters, huh?" He catches up with Bunn who's leading the pack. "Coach Bunn!" He points back. "Is that Hank Luisetti?"

There's more laughter from the team. Bunn cranes his neck back and nods.

Parks waits for Hank and jogs next to him. "You shoot the ball with one hand?"

"We all shoot that way."

They approach a line of cabs and Bunn shouts, "We're headed to the Palestra Arena." He looks at a piece of paper. "It's at 235 South 33rd Street."

Three cabbies jump out of their cars and speedily open doors and trunks.

Bradford, out of breath, asks Hank, "Some people say that's not real basketball."

Hank puts his bag into the trunk of a yellow cab. "If we pop that pea in the can enough times, they might change their tune. After all, you can't throw an opinion through a hoop and put two points on that ol' scoreboard."

Bradford scribbles on his pad as Hank shuts the door, and the cabs pull away. Bradford finishes writing and motions with a finger. "Taxi!"

MADNESS

* * *

FIVE DISHEVELED, FATIGUED boys, dressed in damp, white silk uniforms with cherry red trim, are huddled around their agitated coach midway through the Stanford-Temple match.

The coach, a silver-haired man in a jacket and tie, reprimands them. "You're not focused!"

A black boy, number fifteen, has his hands on his knees and speaks in winded tones, "It's hard to focus..." He takes a breath and adds, "When our fans are cheering for the other team."

A boy wiping sweat off his face with a towel, number six, says, "That Luisetti kid is all over the place."

Number twelve shoots him a look. "So guard him, fool!"

Number six crosses to number twelve. "Who are you calling—"

The coach gets between them. "Double-team him!"

A jarring whistle sends them onto the court where Hank, Art, Spook, Dinty, and Howie are in position. Number six, covered by Howie, inbounds the ball. Six attempts a pass to number twelve, but Hank flies in and scoops it out of the air. The fans roar approval, hoping to see another spectacular one-handed shot. Hank snakes his way forward, and number twelve leaves Howie to double-team Hank. Hank leaps high in the air and hooks a pass to Howie who shoots and scores. The Philly crowd cheers. Ned Irish sits unnoticed in the throng of people. His wooden nature suffocates any emotional expression, but his eyes are glued on Stanford's star forward, whose addictive aura cast a spell over thousands of Philadelphia faithfuls.

* * *

STANFORD DISCHARGES FOUR days of pent-up energy at the Palestra Arena, but it's Hank who is at the helm. After his third one-handed shot, a forty-foot stunner that barely kisses the net, the game is virtually over. The Owls realize they're playing with someone who is well beyond their scope, and the crowd marvels at his unique athleticism. For them, it turns into a show.

The Indians blow out one of the best team in the east, barely breaking a sweat. They leave the Palestra Arena, laughing, loose, and confident—perhaps, a little too confident.

CHAPTER TWENTY-ONE

THE SLURRING SOUND of a slow-motion film clip has Carmela rushing to crank the handle on the Victrola, and the song "Hark! The Herald Angels Sing" soon becomes recognizable. She walks back to the table and places lasagna noodles in a baking dish. Amalia is talking to Hank on the telephone, who is sitting on his bed in a hotel room in Philadelphia with the door ajar.

"Which-a one?" Amalia asks.

"The Philadelphia Tribune, but they changed their tune after they saw us play."

John Bunn peeks in the doorway and mouths, "We have to go."

Hank nods. "I have to go, Mom. Write down the name of the New York hotel."

"Hold-a the line." She throws her voice in the direction of the kitchen. "Stefano, bring-a the pence!"

Stefano enters with a pencil and paper.

Amalia hands the phone to him. "It's-a you son."

Hank's heart shoots into his throat.

Amalia leaves the receiver on the table and helps Carmela with the lasagna.

Stefano grasps the phone. "Buon Natale, Angelo!"

"Pop? Oh... Merry Christmas! Uh... oh, it's the a... Edison Hotel at 228 West 47th Street."

Stefano talks and writes. "It's 228 West..." Stefano clears his throat. "How's you trip? You in-a newspaper again? That's-a nice."

143

Hank's heart slides back into place. "Thanks, Pop!"

Dinty enters the room and sees Hank beaming. He whispers, "Bunn's getting fidgety."

Hank nods and Dinty leaves. "Hey Pop, I've got to go. The coach is waiting."

"You travel on-a Christmas?"

"No, we're all going out to eat. Pop, I really have to run. I'll call tonight. Tell Nonna I said goodbye... Thanks, and Merry Christmas to you too." Hank hangs up the phone, leaps in the air, and runs out the door.

Stefano hangs-up and runs his hands through his hair. He feels the weight of Amalia's stare, and he turns to see his wife looking at him with tears running down her cheeks. Amalia races over and hugs him.

* * *

ON THE MORNING of December 26, Stanford is back at the West Philadelphia Railroad Station. They are on their way to Washington D.C. for their exhibition game against the Georgetown Hoyas. John Bunn sits with his hat over his eyes, on a bench. H.B. Lee and Sparky rest on the same bench. Phil Zonne sits next to H.B. and reads from an open newspaper. "LIU Notches 43rd Straight!"

The remainder of the team, surrounded by Parks, Bradford, and four other reporters, are close by, trying to roll oranges into a cocked hat. Art rolls an orange toward the hat but misses.

"You boys put on quite a show the other night," a reporter says and points to Hank. "Especially him."

Howie takes a shot at the hat, and it lands just in front of the target.

MADNESS

Dinty moves the hat a little farther back and says, "My turn! Watch it and weep, boys!" Dinty rolls an orange. It hits the hat but rolls past it. He crumbles. "That was so close!"

A reporter walks over to Bunn who's still resting his eyes. He clears his throat to get Bunn's attention. "Excuse me, Mr. Bunn. I'm curious about something. Do you have set plays?"

Bunn sits upright and rubs his eyes. "We go where the ball is."

The reporter scribbles. "So instead of playing the man, you play the ball?"

The faint sound of a train is heard.

Bunn rises. "That's correct. Gather up your gear, boys!"

Spook scoops up an orange. "This, gentlemen, is for all the oranges." With exaggerated, slapstick motions, he rolls an orange and it plops into the hat. He does a back handspring and knocks over a garbage can. Most everyone laughs.

Not amused, a cigar-smoking reporter asks, "Do you guys always joke around?"

Hank answers, "Pretty much!"

Cigar Smoker adds with a sarcastic bite, "Your meeting with LIU may be a sobering experience. They're not Temple, y'know."

Hank smiles and references Cal who were clobbered by LIU. "And we're not the Bears."

The train pulls in as Spook gathers the oranges into a brown bag. He looks at Bradford. "Mr. Bradford, if, in five seconds, you can think of three words that rhyme with orange, you can have the bag."

Bradford thinks.

Spook walks toward the train. "Onne, twoo—Mm! These smell divine—thrree, fourr, five. Time's up!"

John Bunn smiles as the team boards.

Parks, shaking his head, looks at Bradford. "Pat, nothing rhymes with orange."

The reporters laugh, even Cigar Guy. Bradford smiles and shakes his fist at Spook who's looking at Bradford through the window while peeling an orange. Spook waves to the reporters as the train pulls away.

* * *

ON TUESDAY, DECEMBER 29, the Blackbirds sit around a table at Grossinger's Country Club in the Catskills.

Irving reads aloud from a newspaper: "The status of West Coast hoops skyrocketed after Chief Hank Luisetti and his tribe slaughtered the Owls on Christmas Eve."

Jules bites a piece of bread and throws the remainder of it on the table.

Irving continues, "Every man on Stanford towers over six foot three, and their newfangled style proved a curve ball to the traditional-bound eastern paradigm. The team was dubbed 'The Laughing Boys' by the Philadelphia press due to their carefree play and off-court antics. LIU may have their hands full when Hank Luisetti rides into the Garden intent on stringing another bird to the back of his horse."

Hillhouse snarls. "Laughing boys, huh? Pretty soon, they'll be laughing out their asses."

* * *

AFTER SPEAKING WITH Stefano, Hank has a bounce in his step. In some ways, he'd been like Scrooge's business partner, Jacob Marley, who was condemned for leading a sinful life. He had to walk the earth alone as a ghost for all eternity, fettered in thick chains that dragged along the ground like a bride's train. Hank condemned himself with the guilt of choosing to follow his own dreams instead of his father's dreams for him. One place where he feels free is on the court; however, the shackles always return when the game ends. In essence, basketball has been both the illness and cure. There are moments when he is able to wriggle free of himself, like when he decided to attend Stanford. But he hasn't fully expelled his demons. He hasn't become the man his mother told him he was when he first left for college. The chains of expectations, the future, and his own identity plague him, and some of his heaviest links are Connie. He built a wall between him and her for self-preservation, but with Stefano's change of heart, he feels a prodigious sense of relief, and the wall protecting Hank from Connie begins to crack.

* * *

STANFORD SCRIMMAGES THE Hoyas in a private facility on December 26 and practice at the same location for the next two days. They will arrive in Manhattan on December 29, have dinner at a New York diner, and enjoy a relaxing evening in the hotel. The boys are brimming with excitement when they arrive, and John Bunn agrees on a quick detour to the Empire State Building before daylight disappears. With their three yellow cabs parked a few feet away, they stand at the base of the tallest building in the world and look up in awe:

"Pictures do it no justice," Hank says, looking up.

Art exclaims, "It's hard to believe we're really here."

"I don't know about you guys, but I'm getting dizzy," Dinty says, rubbing his forehead.

H.B. elbows him. "Tell me you wouldn't climb up there

like King Kong if Fay Wray were waiting at the top."

"Hmm… I might, when you put it that way."

One of the waiting cabbies rolls down his window and shouts to Bunn, "I'm not a tour bus. Let's get a move on, bub!"

Spook shouts back, "It's Bunn to you, sir!"

Bunn rustles Spook's hair.

Howie, rocking back and forth, says, "I agree with that guy. It's freezing out here!"

Phil agrees, "Sounds good to me."

"I can feel the cold through the soles of my shoes," Sparky says, jogging in place.

A ten-year-old newsy, wearing a shabby coat and cap, sells papers across the street. His legs are encased in bulky metal braces. He shouts in a high-pitched voice, "President Roosevelt pushes NRA!"

Hank notices the boy, and thoughts of skyscrapers, cabs, and Madison Square Garden, are replaced by scenes of Hank at the docks with his dad, Ricky Durán giving him a special gift, and a lumbering journey across a puddled, dilapidated playground. A pack of teens jogs behind the newsy, and a foot juts out sweeping the boy's ankle. Laughter and detached newspapers mushroom in the air above the fallen boy and disperse in the chill New York air. Hank bolts across the street oblivious to traffic. Horns blow and cars screech.

Bunn shouts, "Hank!"

Hank runs to the boy, still on his back, and helps him to his feet. "You okay?"

The boy nods with closed eyes and a bowed head. Hank picks up the boy's cap, brushes it off, and hands it to him. John Bunn and the rest of the team join them and chase down papers blowing away in the wind.

As he slides on his cap, the newsy looks at Hank. He

scrunches his face in concentration then his eyes and mouth spring open in an animated 'aha' moment. "Hey, you're that basketball player from California! I see your picture in the papers." The boy's baby blues pan the protective wall of gigantic smiling Indians that's formed around him. Each member of the Stanford team hands him a few sheets of runaway newspapers.

Dinty says, "I think we got most of them."

Hank smiles as he playfully taps the brim of the boy's cap and puts out his hand. "Take care now."

The boy shakes Hank's hand and says in his high-pitched voice, "I hope you win tomorrow!"

Hank crouches down next to him. "You have a pretty tight grip. You know that?"

"I carry papers around the streets every day!"

"What's your name?"

"Wally O'Connor."

"Do you play basketball, Wally?"

Wally points to his braces. "I'd like to but..."

Hank takes out his wallet and removes the old family photo of him as a boy with the braces and bamboo fishing pole. He points to himself. "That's me."

Art and Dinty look at each other, and Bunn raises his eyebrows. Wally looks at the photo, then at Hank, and a dimpled smile slowly spreads across his round, freckled face.

The cabbie blows his horn. "C'mon, bub."

Spook yells back, "I told you. It's B—"

Bunn cuts him off. "That's enough, Jack."

"Would you like to come to the game tomorrow night?" Hank asks the boy. "We have two great seats."

Hank looks at Bunn who taps his back pocket, pulls out his wallet, and produces Dr. Elliot's tickets.

Wally gasps. "Oh boy! Can I bring my uncle Max?"

"You can bring anyone you want."

Hank takes the tickets from Bunn and winks as he hands them to Wally. The boy watches his hero lead his crew back to the waiting vehicles. As they depart, arms shoot out of open windows and wave to their little friend. Wally waves his arm high and sweeps it left to right like a metronome. His little body, up on his toes, turns to the moving caravan until they are swallowed up in a sea of cars flowing along Eighth Avenue.

CHAPTER TWENTY-TWO

A WELL-DRESSED CLERK, with slicked-back hair and a trimmed mustache, hands John Bunn a set of keys. Hank and Dinty stand to Bunn's right. The rest of the team received their keys already and were en route to their rooms. The square-shaped lobby of the Edison Hotel features two ornate floor vases that house meticulously pruned trees, on either side of the front entrance, and a large oil painting of Thomas Edison behind the desk.

Ricky Durán, Eddie, in a Marine Corps uniform, Yang, Mac, and Mario enter the hotel.

Eddie yells out, "Hank!"

He spins around, opens his mouth in a wide "O," and runs to his Galileo friends where he is greeted with hugs, handshakes, and slaps on the back. The clerk glances up at the ruckus with one raised eyebrow and shakes his head.

Hank breaks away and pulls Dinty into the circle. "I want you all to meet my buddy Dinty Moore." He points to Bunn. "And my coach, John Bunn."

Everyone exchanges pleasantries.

Bunn asks Durán, "How was your trip, Ricky?"

The boys move into a corner away from the snobbish glances of the clerk.

Ricky replies, "Fine. We checked-in this morning and went sightseeing for the day."

"It's a grand place, but I don't think me and the missus could ever live here," Bunn says.

"I like its energy," says Ricky.

"It's a young man's city, I guess! If you'll excuse me, I'm gonna get settled in." The two men shake and Bunn waves. "Nice meeting you all."

Dinty turns to the guys and says, "I'm going up too. I wanted to use a bathroom in the subway and decided it'd be better to wait. You should have seen that thing."

"Thanks for the warning!" Hank says.

Everyone laughs.

Dinty waves. "Nice meeting you!" He grabs Hank's suitcase and leaves with Bunn.

Hank looks at his friends, shakes his head, and says, "I can't believe you guys are here!"

"You'll never guess who else is," Eddie says.

Mario playfully adds, "He'll never guess."

Hank freezes.

Eddie, with a boyish grin, says, "Go to room 444 and find out."

Hank remains frozen.

Eddie lightly punches Hank. "Stop it with that face. You're gonna love this, Hank. Trust me."

Hank's mouth defrosts. "Who is it?"

"Room 444, Hank. Go!"

He walks and then runs to the elevator and smacks the 'up' button like the firing of a machine gun. When the door opens, he rushes in before allowing a woman to exit—another raised eyebrow.

Hank fixes his hair on the way up and jumps out sideways when the door opens. He looks at the directional plate on the wall and hangs a sharp right. As he gets closer, he slows and stops short in front of 444. He smells the air and puts his ear against the door. Someone walks out of room 446 and Hank jumps. He knocks on 444 and smiles at the couple who half-smile at him as they walk by.

He hears footsteps and finally a voice, "Who's-a there?"

"Pop?"

The door opens, and Stefano flings his arms open. "Angelo!"

Amalia rushes over, hugs Hank, and drags him into the room.

"Why didn't you tell me?"

Stefano says, "It's a surprise!"

Amalia and Stefano take turns telling Hank how they traveled to New York with Ricky and the neighborhood kids and that it was Stefano who planned the surprise.

"You father look at-a me and say, 'Amalia, we goin' to New York.'"

Stefano, with the energy of his youth, says, "Nonna said, 'I watch the business.'"

"Dante is going to hate me!" Hank says with a rubbery grimace.

They all laugh and spend the next hour talking.

Finally, Hank leaves his chair and says, "I'd better get unpacked. I have a big day tomorrow."

"You wanna stay here?" Stefano asks. "We have-a space."

"No thanks, Pop. I have a room upstairs with a teammate."

They approach the door. Hank opens it and turns back to his smiling parents.

Stefano takes Hank's hands. "I'm-a so proud of you, Angelo." Stefano kisses his son on both cheeks and follows it with a long embrace. Hank squeezes his eyes closed and locks his chin over Stefano's shoulder. They both wipe away tears when they let go.

Hank hugs Amalia and says, "I'll see you tomorrow."

Amalia and Stefano smile and watch Hank walk down the hall until he is out of view. The closer Hank gets to the elevator the faster he walks, then jogs, then runs. He stops at the elevator but doesn't wait for it to arrive. He sees the stairwell door, rips it open, and pops in. He runs up three flights of stairs, two steps at a time.

* * *

WRAPPED IN A towel, Dinty opens the door. As Hank walks in, Dinty makes his way to the bathroom.

"In a few minutes, you'd have been stuck out there."

The moment Dinty closes the door, Hank grabs the phone. It rings at the D'Angelo residence just as Connie passes by. She enters the room to answer it, and as she picks up the receiver, Serafina comes bustling in.

Connie, speaking into the phone says, "Hold the line, please."

Serafina whines, "But I wanted to get it. I'm telling Daddy!" She runs out of the room.

Connie speaks into the phone, "Hello?"

"Serafina hasn't changed a bit, has she?"

Connie closes her eyes tightly and grips her forehead with an open palm. Her expression relaxes, but her eyes remain closed. She nearly whispers, "Hello, Hank."

Hank smiles and shakes his head slowly. "I can't tell you how it feels to hear your voice. I miss you so much Connie. I've got to see you as soon as I get back home..." Hank responds to the phone, "Oh, you heard?"

Connie puts down the phone base and buries her face in her hand.

The silence cools Hank's heart and releases the first rotation of churning stomach acid. "Connie?"

She pulls her hand from her face, regains her composure, and raises her voice. "Now, Hank? After eight months? I asked everyone if you called after I got home from the train that night, and when you didn't, I thought maybe they missed it. So I slept next to the phone and waited the whole next day. I waited and waited and waited. You were a few minutes away from me all summer long, and you never called or came by. After a year and a half, you just stopped calling me? After all we said to each other, all the time we spent together, and all the trips to watch you play, you didn't call me?"

Hank holds the phone base with white knuckles. "Connie, please forgive me. Please! Tell me you still love me! You have got to tell me you still love me!"

Connie wipes away tears, and the lamp reflects light off her diamond ring. "Gerard proposed to me last month." She closes her eyes and hangs her head. "Why did you do this, Hank? Why? Please don't ever call me again." As Connie slowly hangs up the receiver, the mousy sound of Hank's voice is heard calling out from the phone.

"Connie? Con—"

She hangs up and falls to her knees, crying into the palms of her hands. The bedroom door swings open, and Connie's father rushes in. She springs up and smacks into him, clamping on tightly. His shoulder muffles guttural sobs rolling out in gravelly bursts.

Hank stares as blankly as he had that night at the train station. The phone drops out of his hand and crashes onto the floor. He lies down on the bed, face up, expressionless. Tears slip out of the corners of his eyes, stream past his ears, and disappear into his hair.

He turns on his side and pretends to sleep when he hears

Dinty exiting the bathroom. Dinty picks up the phone and puts it back in its place. He studies Hank for a few beats, and then shuts the light and climbs into bed. Hank's eyes are fixed on the wall for hours before his infamous night demons attack. He jumps out of bed panicked and laboring for air. His hand squeezes his chest while he paces to and fro.

Dinty leaps up. "What's the matter?"

Hank takes a few deep breaths before answering, "Bad dream." He wipes sweat off his forehead.

"You scared the crap out of me, buddy."

"I'm okay. It was just a bad dream."

Dinty says, "Go wash your face, and you'll be good as new." Dinty watches Hank walk into the bathroom and climbs back into bed when he hears the water running.

Hank leans on the sink with his hands and looks in the mirror. He jumps to turn on the shower then flushes the toilet as he grabs a folded towel, puts it over his face, and screams into it. His knees bend and he crumples to the floor, the side of his face flat against the tile under the toilet. He presses the towel back to his face and screams into it again, the second in a series of outbursts that leave him limp and weary. The warm mist of the shower mixes with salty tears and sweat while he shivers on the cold tile floor.

* * *

THE CARTOONIST LOOKS at his picture of a blackbird with its wings spread, standing behind a nest filled with numbered eggs stacked in a pyramid. One prominent egg, number forty-three, sits in front. He scratches an unrecognizable signature on the bottom right corner.

AN EARMUFFED NEWSY, with fingerless gloves, hawks papers in front of Madison Square Garden on the morning of December 30. The cartoonist's illustration is spread across the back page.

Cloudy puffs of condensation accompany the newsy's words, "Indians invade New York. Read all about it! It happens tonight right here at the Garden!"

A man with a wool scarf and a red nose hands a nickel to the newsy who takes three pennies from a satchel and hands them to the man.

The newsy tips his hat. "Thank-you, sir." He continues his sales pitch to the hordes of bundled-up New Yorkers, "Blackbirds defend their forty-three-game streak. East or West, who's it gonna be?"

CHAPTER TWENTY-THREE

JOHN BUNN POUNDS on Hank and Dinty's door. Hank lies there open eyed on the bed. Dinty flies up and lets him in.

"Time to get up. I called several times."

Dinty looks at the phone and back at John. "I think the phone might be broken."

Bunn hopes to keep his team loose until game time, so he plans their meals and builds a sightseeing schedule around Central Park, Rockefeller Center, and FAO Schwartz. Hank tells Bunn he is spending the day with his folks, and he tells his folks that he has to spend the day with the team.

Hank wants to be alone.

When he and Connie broke up eight months ago, he longed to be with people so he could take his mind off Connie. But after last night, he simply gives up. He no longer has the will or strength to fight. Whether it is because he hardly slept or that he always thought they would reconcile at some point, the finality of the phone call breaks him. Hank spends the day lying on his back. He attempts to assuage the pain by thinking of the future, how he will resolve this, and the things he will say to Connie, Dinty, his parents, Coach Bunn, Ricky Durán, and Eddie, but nothing slows the swirling circular thoughts. Each parasitic rotation consumes his energy, but sleep refuses to take him. Hank has no desire to eat or drink or talk or pace, only to lie there in his dark room fighting phantoms.

* * *

IN THE BROADCAST booth at Madison Square Garden sits Joel Hall, a balding man in his sixties, wearing red and blue checkered suspenders and a matching bowtie over a white button-down shirt. He's with Alan Bloom, a man in his forties with a black goatee wearing a tailored, pinstriped blue suit. Both men sport large earphones and have a fat, oblong microphone set before them. A technician walks in the booth and the two men look at him. He looks at his wristwatch, slowly raises his index finger, and points at Hall.

"Welcome to Madison Square Garden. I'm Joel Hall, and I'm here tonight for the pregame show with sports analyst, Alan Bloom."

Bloom leans into the microphone. "Good evening, Ladies and Gentlemen."

Hall looks at Bloom. "I could hardly wait to get here tonight. Our lineup has been the talk of the town for at least a week. In the first contest, NYU tries to avenge last year's heartbreaking loss to Georgetown. The main event features a Titanic battle of East/West champions as the Long Island University Blackbirds, winners of forty-three consecutive games, take on the reigning Pacific Coast Champion Stanford Indians!"

Bloom smirks. "They play a different brand of basketball out west. It's a bit peculiar if you ask me."

Hall points to Bloom. "And their nicknames are just as quirky. There's Jack "Spook" Calderwood, Bryan "Dinty" Moore—"

"He must like stew."

Hall chuckles. "I would assume so. Then there's Hank Luisetti, whose real name is Angelo Giuseppe Luisetti. How do you get Hank from Angelo?"

"Maybe Hank is an English translation of Angelo."

"Maybe."

* * *

COPS STRUGGLE TO organize the mob, forcing themselves into Madison Square Garden.

A man gasps as the wind is pushed out of him. "If the players take this much abuse, it'll be the game of the century."

A cop runs to his patrol car to call for backup. "We need more uniforms at Madison Square Garden right now! It's a damned stampede over here!"

* * *

ON THE GYM floor, Nat Holman is surrounded by scribbling reporters. He bellows, "I'll quit coaching if I have to teach one-handed shots to win. They'll have to show me plenty to convince me that a shot predicted on a prayer is smart basketball. There's only one way to shoot, and that's the way we do it in the east—with two hands!"

* * *

JOEL HALL TALKS into the mic, "All of New York is abuzz about Stanford's Eye-talian sharpshooter, Hank Luisetti, spawned from the same neighborhood as Yankee superstars DiMaggio, Lazzeri and Crosetti, and the only player in hoops history to score fifty points in one game."

* * *

IN THE LOCKERS below, Hank sits listlessly in his street clothes on a bench away from the rest of the group. He gazes downward with bloodshot eyes.

Spook, Howie, and Dinty sit on a bench around ten feet from Hank.

Spook takes a pair of high topped, black leather, red laced athletic shoes out of a box and displays a shoe on his hand. "State of the art equipment, my friends. Smell that leather." He sticks the shoe under Dinty's nose.

Dinty pushes it away. "Cut it out you lunatic."

"Ahh, the ugly face of jealousy."

"It's going to be the bloody face of Calderwood if you stick that thing in my face again!"

Howie observes Hank. "Hey Dint, Hank doesn't look so good. Is he all right?"

Dinty looks over and then back at Howie. "He's been like that since last night. But you know Hank, he'll be fine once he steps on the court."

Spook stands. "Perhaps a whiff of these fine athletic shoes will bring him around."

Dinty pulls him down by the arm. "I think he could do without that."

"Another jealous teammate," says Spook with his nose in the air.

* * *

NUMEROUS POLICEMEN WITH long winter coats have organized the mob outside the Garden into a steady moving line. Wally and Uncle Max, a man in his forties with a handlebar mustache and wool longshoreman cap, are among the crowd.

* * *

MADNESS

JOEL HALL LOOKS at Alan Bloom with a sarcastic smile. "Jack Mahon of the Daily News said, and I quote, 'Stanford is accorded a good chance to upset the fast-stepping Blackbirds,' end quote."

Bloom's rubbery grimace and head shaking reveals his feelings on the subject.

The technician comes in and points to his watch.

"That comes from a man who knows that this is the best Blackbird team of the streak. Of LIU's ten victories this year, they've beaten their opponents by an average of twenty-eight points. Some teams don't even score twenty-eight points in a game. Alan, you were at the Stanford/Temple game. Do you agree with this sentiment?"

Bloom swipes at the air in disgust. "The Birds will riddle these guys. Stanford doesn't have set plays and no discernible discipline. They gang the man with the apple! That's schoolyard ball. They're not even in LIU's league."

Hall shrugs. "We'll soon see what these guys are all about and if LIU could contain Stanford's All-American forward, Hank Luisetti."

While looking at his watch, the technician holds up his two fists and flicks up one finger at a time, mouthing up to ten.

Hall looks at the technician while addressing the mic. "That's the end of our pregame show. I'd like to thank Alan Bloom for joining us this evening."

"It's always a pleasure Joel. I look forward to a spectacular evening of basketball."

"And now a word from our sponsor."

* * *

AFTER A FINAL tactical meeting, John Bunn is being interviewed while the rest of the team is dressed in their uniforms and talking in pockets around the room. Dinty, Howie, and Art pass a ball to each other. Hank, in uniform, sits on a bench while he gets his ankles taped by the Garden physician, Dr. Aldrik, a bald man in his late sixties.

Distant cheers and vibrations trickle down like rain from the ceiling.

* * *

AMALIA, STEFANO, RICKY, Eddie, and the rest of the Galileo team, talk cheerfully from their third-row center seats, compliments of John Bunn.

Pat Bradford and Eric Parks chat with several cameramen on the sidelines.

In the home-team locker room, Clair Bee addresses his team seated in a semicircle. He is flanked by Abe Tanenbaum on his right and Ira Schwartz on his left.

Bee speaks with crisp intensity, "You represent New York. You are the East Coast champs, and after tonight, virtual national champions." He slowly scratches his face with his ring finger. "This is your crowd, your family, your house, your city. After tonight, you will be royalty!"

Jules Bender looks around at his teammates, nodding. Hillhouse wipes sweat from his brow.

Hall touches the mic from behind. "NYU played 'em tough but wound up on the short end of a 36-30 score. I really thought we were going to catch them toward the end. Even though we lost, it was a thoroughly entertaining game."

* * *

MADNESS

IN THE VISITING locker room, John Bunn and his players are laughing at Spook's performance of Howie sleeping. Spook lies on a bench with saliva dripping out of his mouth while mimicking long, exaggerated snores.

After a particularly guttural snort, Spook gets up. "Ow!" He rubs his nose. "I think I might have pulled a sinus muscle."

Hank is in the bathroom dousing his face with water. He pats his skin with a towel and walks into the room where Spook is bowing.

A short, black man, Willie Williams, wearing a wool cap, enters the room and shouts out, "It's game time, fellas. Follow me."

The smile disappears from Bunn's face. "Okay, boys. Let's go!"

The team follows Bunn. Hank, the last to leave, sighs and exits the room. His feet become sandbags as he struggles to keep pace with his teammates who are waiting for him at the entranceway. John Bunn takes a step toward Hank but is interrupted by Willie Williams, who addresses the team with the exaggerated movements of a traffic cop.

"I'm going to walk out and wave to the announcer, see..." He taps his chest. "When I get the sign, I'll call on you to come out. When you come out, line up along the half-court line near the ref, see..." Willie enters the court, waves to the booth, then calls Stanford onto the court with roundhouse arm rotations. "Let's go! Let's go! It's time!"

The Garden announcer's megaphoned voice rattles over the screaming fans, "Ladies and Gentlemen... The West Coast Champion, Stanford Indians!"

The Stanford team is punched with boos as they jog onto the court. A roll of toilet paper hits Art in the head and the crowd cheers. As Hank jogs out, he looks up and sees a giant

165

neon sign and thousands of small flickering lights. The flickering lights focus into cigarettes. Through a haze of smoke, he sees rows and rows of people as far and as high as he can see. The humbled Stanford team lines up along the half-court line.

Wally, sitting second row center directly in front of Ricky Durán's crew, stands and points to Hank. "That's him, Uncle Max, number seven!"

Stefano's shoulders and chin are lifted high with pride as he looks to Amalia. "That's-a my Angelo!"

Amalia smiles and hooks her arm around his.

Cheers and whistling rise just after the announcer's introduction. "Let's hear it for the winners of forty-three consecutive games…" Deafening cheers smother his words, "…the East Coast Champ—"

The Blackbirds glide out with swagger in their black-satin uniforms and face off opposite the Indians. A referee wearing a navy blue and white striped shirt runs out with two basketballs. LIU is amused by the Indians' jitters. Jules looks directly into Hank's vacant eyes.

The ref busts out his orders, "You're free to run your warmups as you like, but when I blow the whistle twice, go over and line up along your foul line." He hands Jules and Hank a ball and each team jogs away.

Hillhouse turns to Irving. "They're a-scared."

"Like huckleberries in Bensonhoist, Artie."

All laugh except Jules.

Stanford jogs to their half amidst heckling and boos.

Spook looks around at the feral fans. "You think we'll make it out of here alive?"

Howie nods. "I was wondering that myself. They're the wildest bunch I've ever seen."

When the Indians get in positions for their warm-ups,

MADNESS

Hank stands next to Dinty and rubs sweat off his face with his shirt.

"You okay, buddy?"

Hank nods. Bunn scratches his head on the sideline as he looks at Hank.

CHAPTER TWENTY-FOUR

IN THE BROADCAST booth, Hall focuses on the Indians. "I don't know what they're feeding those boys, but it's like they're playing with five centers. They must have something more than just height, by the way they ran through Temple. Rumor has it they beat up on the Hoyas too."

* * *

THE CARTOONIST SITS in a hazy press box where a long, rectangular table of reporters gab. Each man is perched in front of a telephone and a heavy, black manual typewriter loaded with a clean sheet of white paper. The cartoonist feeds the foggy air with a series of sleepy smoke rings before pulling a pencil case from his briefcase and placing it on the table near his typewriter.

* * *

NED IRISH SITS courtside with John Reed Kilpatrick and Nat Holman. Brian Hurley walks over and hands Ned a note: "Attendance 17,623, the largest of the year." Ned smiles.

* * *

HALL LEANS INTO the mic. "Alan Bloom and I had a discussion during the commercial break, and I said I think we're going to have a game. Alan disagreed saying, 'I wouldn't care who they beat, how tall they are, or if Hercules was their start-ing center, LIU has the best basketball team in history, and they will go undefeated this year.'"

* * *

HANK LABORS THROUGH the warmups, and John Bunn watches with concern as his All-American forward misses two attempts from the foul line. Bunn starts to jog onto the court and is turned around by two blasts of a piercing whistle. The teams line up along the foul line and the lights dim. A sharp, white spotlight burns a circle in the center of the half-court line, where a gray-bearded man dressed in a tuxedo wraps his hands around a free-standing microphone. The Garden stands, the players put their hands over their hearts, and the opening notes of "The Star-Spangled Banner" fills the silence of the hushed arena. The singer drones on, but neither the lyrics nor the melody are absorbed by the disjointed Indi-ans. While Hank may be physically and emotionally ex-hausted, the rest of the tribe has been stunned into submission from the minute they emerged through the doors behind Wil-lie Williams. The Garden is the Colosseum and the Indians are the convicts who would receive a thumbs up or down if they survive the battle. After the singer croons the last note, cheers and houselights flare. The teams jog to their coaches. When they arrive, Bunn feels their apprehension, and he assumes Hank has a case of anxiety like the rest of his boys.

Bunn plays it cool. "Just play the game and have some fun. Ya got that?"

There are a few nods, but for the most part apathy stares back at him.

Bunn, with a harder edge, says, "I didn't hear ya!"

The team responds in unison with a simultaneous clap and a "Yes!"

"Now go out there and show 'em what ya got!"

Dinty, Howie, Spook, Art, and Hank jog onto the court. Bunn rubs his chin as his boys move into position. The Galileo crew cheers. Eddie glances at Stefano and smiles as if to say, "Wait until you see your son," Wally, holding a hot dog, follows Hank with his eyes. The two teams meet at half-court. Paired circularly around Art Stoefen and Art Hillhouse are Hank and Jules, Dinty and Irving, Howie and Myron, and Spook and Danny.

Hall's voice comes over the loudspeaker: "The ball is lowered between the centers. The big guys ready themselves... and away we go. Art Hillhouse taps it to Irving Torgoff who dribbles and dishes to Dan Kaplowitz. He fires to Jules Bender, wide open near the foul line. Bender sets, shoots, and scores a banker."

Bedlam breaks out from the stands.

"And just like that, the Birds are up, two-zip." Hall puts up two fingers. "Stanford didn't see the ball until it fell through the hoop. Hank Luisetti inbounds the ball and passes to Bryan Moore, who brings it up. Moore passes to Luisetti who crosses the foul line, fakes, and shoots a one-handed shot. The ball ricochets inside the rim and pops out."

The audience cheers.

"Hillhouse pulls down the rebound and hands off to Jules Bender, who takes it up. Bender crosses the foul line, turns, sets, shoots, scores. It's four-nothing. Birds!"

* * *

MADNESS

HANK IS WORKING on muscle memory alone. He's trying to shake off the mental haze, but his arms and legs are encased in steel, and the vise squeezing his head presses harder each time he moves.

Watching Hank, Hall says, "Luisetti inbounds the ball to Spook Calderwood who flips to Howie Turner. He drives to the middle and gets stopped by Hillhouse in the lane. Turner leaps and slings it around Hillhouse to Luisetti who has an open shot… but he doesn't shoot. He's now pressed hard by Bender."

Eddie says to Ricky Durán, "What's he doing? I've seen him make that shot a thousand times."

Hall says, "Luisetti makes his way up to the foul line and shovels off to Spook Calderwood. He passes to Howie Turner who shoots and misses. Hillhouse gets aggressive under the basket and pulls down the rebound."

Bunn, red faced, yells out, "Watch the pushing, Ref!"

Hall follows the action. "Hillhouse hands off to Jules Bender who brings it up. Bender dishes to Irving Torgoff, covered aggressively by Luisetti. Torgoff slings it to Dan Kaplowitz who zips it to Hillhouse. He feeds Jules, but Calderwood gets a hand on it and tips it to Luisetti at the top of the key." Hall stands. "Luisetti dribbles all alone toward the goal, steps into the layup… and misses! Oh my. The ball rolled off the back of the rim."

Wally covers his eyes.

Stefano turns to Amalia. "What's-a the matter with Angelo?"

Nat Holman elbows Ned Irish who keeps his eyes fixed on the game. "What did I tell you, Ned? The one-handed wonder. Why, he can't even hit a layup!"

* * *

MOMENTUM, THE FICKLE arm of fate, has the power to give or take away. Sometimes it fancies the underdog and other times it shows no mercy. Tonight, it is watching the game from the LIU bench, munching on a New York hot dog, and enjoying the view. Every single Blackbird is playing the game of his life. Five players are gelling together while executing every nuance of the game to perfection: passing, rebounding, dribbling, stealing, and shooting.

Irving scores.

Jules scores.

Eddie squirms.

Clair Bee cheers.

Myron scores.

Hall is practically eating the mic, "Hillhouse muscles a rebound from Spook, jumps up, shoots, and scores! Art Hillhouse is a one-man-wrecking machine tonight."

Bradford looks at Parks, perplexed. Spook steps out of bounds and the ref blows his whistle, slightly longer than necessary.

John Bunn makes a "T" with his hands. "Time!"

"And the Indians call time," Hall says. "The massacre, no pun intended, will return shortly."

Dinty, Spook, Howie, Art, and Hank lumber over to John Bunn, who assumes the stance of an irate parent waiting for a child to explain his abysmal behavior. When they gather round him, they look everywhere but his glowering face.

Bunn throws his arms wide. "Can someone tell me what in Sam Hill is going on out there? Twelve to zero?" Bunn turns his attention to his star forward. "Hank, are you ill, son?"

Hank's shining face is dripping wet, and he wipes it with his soaked shirt.

Bunn puts his hand on Hank's shoulder. "If you're not well, I have to pull you."

Hank looks at his teammates and then at Bunn. "I'm fine."

The coach looks at his players. "Does anyone have anything they want to tell me?"

Some respond, "No." Others shake their heads.

Bunn takes a long, deep breath, smiles, and speaks with paternal affection, "Okay, let's start over. I don't care about winning. All I want to do is play them hard and make a game of it. As far as I'm concerned, it's zero to zero, and the game starts now."

At the same time, LIU is gathered around a roused Clair Bee. "He's trying to pump them up as we speak. If you shut them down now, you will break them. Go out there and show them who you are and what you stand for. Let's end this one-handed crap for good!"

The whistle shrieks. Hank breaks from the team and stops near Sparky who is drinking water. He grabs the water, dumps it in a towel, washes it over his head and face, and jogs toward his team.

A small grin appears on Dinty's face just before he says, "Looks like it's going to be a game after all."

The two teams jog on and Jules inbounds the ball. A rejuvenated Stanford covers the Birds tightly. Jules bounce passes it to Irving, but Art gets his hand on it and the ball scurries away.

Hank jets toward the loose ball.

Hillhouse spins around and crashes into Dinty sprinting for the loose ball as well. Hillhouse topples awkwardly backward. As Hank touches the ball, Hillhouse's head smashes into Hank's face. Hank flies back, his head slams against the floor, and blood gushes from above his right eye.

"Luisetti is down, and it doesn't look like he's moving," Hall says. "Since he took the brunt of the hit, he might have been out before he hit the floor."

CHAPTER TWENTY-FIVE

BOTH TEAMS GATHER around Hank. Bunn and Bee arrive just before Dr. Aldrik.

Bunn backs them away with outstretched arms. "Back off. Give him some air!"

The doctor crouches near Hank, straightens the boy's head, and feels for a neck pulse.

Stefano calms his wife. "He's-a fine, Amalia. He's-a strong like a bull."

Eddie chimes in, "Don't you worry, Mrs. Luisetti. He's okay." He lies. "This always happens."

Ricky Durán smiles at Amalia reassuringly, but he and Eddie look at each other, concerned.

John Bunn holds a towel above Hank's eye, and the doctor has his ear to Hank's chest. He then takes a small vial from his shirt pocket, breaks it, and puts it under Hank's nose. He wakes with a sniff.

"How do you feel, son?"

Hank tries to get up, but he's held down by Dr. Aldrik.

"Not so fast. Just lie here for now and look at my hand." The doctor snaps and holds up two fingers. "How many fingers do you see?"

"Three. Can I get up now?"

Howie puts his hand on Dinty's shoulder, and Jules moves the LIU players away.

Hank tries to get up again. "I'm ready to play!"

"Easy now! Your coach and I will help you up and then you're off to the hospital."

Hank's eyes open wide. "Stitch me up in the locker room."

"I'm not so sure that would be the best place for you."

Bunn kneels next to the doctor. "He's a pretty tough kid, Doc."

The doctor looks at the eye again and shrugs, "Okay, but I can't promise that I'll clear him to play."

Bunn nods. "Fair enough."

Hank is helped up by the doctor, and the crowd gives him a standing ovation. He walks across the court holding a bloody towel over his eye.

Bunn walks over to the bench and looks at Phil Zonne. "You're in."

When Hank passes the sideline, he looks up and sees Wally waving to him. Hank hangs his head. Bradford runs over to Hank and pats him on the shoulder. A cameraman attempts a picture of Hank, but Bradford puts his huge hand in front of the lens as the flash pops.

Bradford gives the guy a menacing stare. "Go ahead and try that again, buddy!" and shields Hank until he disappears through a doorway.

Eddie bites the side of his mouth, Ricky Durán stares at the court, Amalia pats under her eyes with a handkerchief, and Stefano blows his nose.

"And fifteen minutes in, Stanford loses its top man," Hall says. "Coach Bunn is in trouble."

Nat Holman looks at Ned Irish. "Hey, what can you do? Maybe next time."

Zonne inbounds the ball and looks for an open man from among the crush of squeaking sneakers mixing it up in front of him. He pitches to Dinty who drives toward the basket. Dinty spots Howie in the right corner and shoots him a one-handed pass. The pass is offline and gives Danny Kaplowitz room to steal. Just as Howie takes possession, he's shouldered by Danny, but he instinctively hooks the ball in the direction of the hoop. The whistle screams. Howie jumps up, and his team charges him.

Howie wrinkles his brow. "Did that thing go in?"

Dinty says, "It sure did."

"Wow!"

The Indians burst out laughing. Spook grabs Howie around the neck and flicks his ear while Bunn smiles from the sidelines.

The Birds look at the laughing Indians as though a spaceship just dropped them onto the court. The ref blasts his whistle, and they jog toward the foul line.

Hillhouse looks at Jules. "They're weird."

As they are jogging, Dinty says, "It's time to start playing our way."

Spook says, "I wish Hank were here."

"We all do," says Dinty.

* * *

IN A SMALL office, Hank lies on his back with his eyes open while Dr. Aldrik pulls a needle through his skin to close the gash. Distant sounds of cheering seep in from under the door. Hank doesn't flinch as the needle takes another pass.

* * *

SPOOK, COVERED BY Jules, dribbles, stops, and flips to Art. He passes to Dinty, who fakes a shot. Irving jumps up. Dinty bends around him and nails a one-hander. Zonne pats Dinty on the backside as he passes by.

"What an outstanding shot!" Hall says.

Hank winces when he hears the painful cheers flowing in from the arena.

Dr. Aldrik places gauze over Hank's eye and puts an ice pack on top of it. "If this gets too cold, take it off for a few minutes, then put it back on." He hands Hank a towel. "These packs tend to leak, so use this if it does."

Hank doesn't respond.

Dr. Aldrik says, "Just give me a nod, son, so I know you're okay."

"I'm fine, Doc."

The doctor walks to the door, opens it, and turns back to Hank. "What's ailing you is much more than some stitches. It's Hank, isn't it?"

He nods.

The doctor walks a little closer and speaks to Hank with a warm smile, "It's always best to let things out, Hank. It clears the soul. I'm just an old fogey, but I've heard many confessions over the past forty years. Oftentimes, a confession works better than whatever tincture I can prescribe."

Hank looks at the doctor. "People have been giving me that advice for months, but I tend to deal with stuff in my own way."

The doc looks at his patient with care. "I understand, Hank. I'll check on you in a bit. Try to get some rest."

As the doctor touches the door, Hank says, "Thanks for not taking me to the hospital… and for everything else too."

"You betcha. Now there's always someone roaming these halls, so just call out if you need something."

After Dr. Aldrik leaves, Hank adjusts the ice pack on his face and closes his eyes, just before slumber pulls him away.

MADNESS

* * *

HANK SMELLS CONNIE before he sees her. When he opens his eyes, he sees her sitting on his left and Gerard sitting next to her on her other side. Hank wonders why he's in Connie's living room. Amalia talks to Connie's mother, the two grandmothers talk in Italian, and Stefano talks to Joseph in the fireplace room. Hank is shivering and looks for a jacket. When he tries to move, he notices that he's a child, and his legs are encased in his old metal braces. Gerard makes a joke, and Connie laughs as she twirls her engagement ring.

* * *

JULES HITS A twenty-five-foot two-hander. Hillhouse scowls and pumps his fist. Thundering cheers shake the walls of the arena.

* * *

HANK'S BODY VIBRATES and the chandelier wiggles. He wants to move, but his braces are bolted to the chair.

He looks over at his mother, but she's rattling on, and then both mothers begin laughing. He wants to talk to Connie, but he can't speak. He tries, but his mouth cannot form words. She puts her arm around Gerard. He kisses her, and they press their foreheads together. Something drips on Hank's head, so he looks up. There are cracks in the ceiling and drops of water seep out.

Ricky Durán is at the table holding the basketball he'd given Hank all those years ago. He is talking with Eddie who's dressed in his Marine Corps uniform. Beside them is a beautiful Filipina with long black hair and red lips, wearing a long red satin dress beaded with gold flowers. Hank tries to get their attention, but Eddie is going on about the Philippines.

Dinty walks in the room, and Connie greets him with a hug. She says it is so nice to see him. He walks past Hank, pulls up a chair, and chats with Eddie, his female friend, and Ricky. John Bunn is there too. Eddie tells the story when he put the girl's underwear sign on Hank's back, and they all burst out laughing. In fact, everyone in the room is laughing or smiling. They are all enjoying themselves.

A sound like strong wind filters in from under the floor. Hank vibrates in his chair, glasses chatter, the chandelier wiggles, and small fragments of plaster fall like sand onto the table. The drops of cold water from above have turned to a trickle and run down his face. Hank finds his voice and cries out, but no one seems to hear him.

He turns to Connie, who is embracing Gerard, and says, "You were right, Connie. You were right about me that day at the train station. When I talked about my future, I was running away from something, but it wasn't you I was running from. It was those words, 'your future.' Those words have always frightened me. I made a mistake, but I couldn't help it. It wasn't that I didn't love you." Tears mix with the water and run down his face. "Why won't you look at me? I love you, Connie!" Hank squeezes his eyes shut and screams from the depths of his soul, "I've loved you since the first moment I saw you!"

Hank takes a few deep breaths through his nose, and he hears Connie's voice.

"I hear you," she says. Connie turns to Hank, cradles his little face with her hands, kisses him on the forehead, smiles, and disappears.

MADNESS

Every person in the room is gone. The only thing left is the old leather basketball sitting on the table in front of him. Hank lunges forward, but it's just beyond the reach of his little fingers. The room vibrates again, sand drops on the table, and the water from above streams down on him. The boy musters every bit of strength and presses all his muscles to their capacity, rocking the chair back and forth. As he strains forward, he is no longer a boy. He is dressed in his Stanford uniform, and his legs are long and strong. A burst of energy erupts in him, and he cries out as he pushes his strength to its limits. A chunk of plaster plops down on the floor next to him. Hank breaks free of the braces and topples onto the floor.

He sits up on the floor of Dr. Aldrik's office. His face is wet, and the melted ice pack lies next to him.

The door flies open and Dr. Aldrik rushes in. "Are you okay? A custodian came running to get me. He heard screaming in here!"

Hank shoots up off the floor, looks Dr. Aldrik dead in his eyes, and says, "You were right, Doc... I'm free of it now!"

The doctor shrugs and says, "I'm glad I could help."

"Thank you," Hank says.

Distant cheers shake the room and glass medical instruments chatter in a cabinet.

Hank shrieks, "What quarter is it?"

"Third."

He bolts toward the door, rips it open with the strength of a lion, looks at the doctor, and says, "You coming?" before he flies out of the room.

CHAPTER TWENTY-SIX

"JULES SINKS A two-handed set shot from the foul line," Hall says. "That's another point for Bender, and the crowd is eating it up. I can't see anyone other than Jules Bender winning the All-American forward honors this year. Bender crouches down. One more, and they will have brought it up to a ten-point lead. He lowers the ball between his legs, flicks it up, and scores! The Birds are up by ten!"

Hank busts onto the court floor and jogs up the sidelines past Wally.

"He's back, Uncle Max! He's back!"

Clair Bee gapes when he sees Hank sprinting toward his coach.

Hank approaches Bunn. "I'm ready, Coach."

Bunn points to the white bandage "Is that okay?"

"I'm cleared."

Dr. Aldrik hustles up the sideline.

Bunn shouts, "Okay?"

The doctor nods, and the Galileo section cheers. Bradford smacks Parks on the back so hard he nearly knocks him over.

Eddie looks at Ricky. "You see that? He had that same look in his eye when he kicked my ass in fourth grade."

Bunn makes a "T" and shouts, "Time out!"

The Indians charge Hank. Spook is the last to arrive and leaps up in a cradle position directly into Hank's arms. "Nice eye."

Clair Bee and his team stare at the Indians, bewildered.

MADNESS

Bee looks at Spook. "There's something wrong with that kid." He motions for his troops to circle around. "Double-team Luisetti. Danny, you cover him to start. Jules, join them in and around the zone."

John Bunn claps his hands and rubs them together. "New strategy, boys. Forget making a game of it. Now, I wanna win it. Hank, it's time to formally introduce yourself to New York."

A whistle blast sends the Indians onto the court.

The referee asks, "Who's inbounding?"

Spook raises his index finger. "I will, sir!"

Danny Kaplowitz looks at Hank towering over him. Fear wriggles up his spine and dings his Adam's apple, triggering a gulp.

Hall hovers over the mic. "Spook Calderwood inbounds the ball to Luisetti, who bursts ahead like a sprinter at the sound of a pistol shot. I've never seen anyone dribble that fast and maintain ball control. Jules Bender sees Luisetti alone and moves toward him head-on. Luisetti accepts the challenge and continues racing toward Bender in a virtual game of chicken. Luisetti moves right, pivots left, leaps in the air, and shoots a one-handed shot, and... it swishes through the net! I've heard about this kid, but it's another thing to see him in action. The crowd actually took a collective gasp on that one."

The Galileo section jumps up and down.

"Did you see that?" Eddie asks Stefano. "Did you see that?"

Ricky kisses Eddie on the cheek. Wally leaps up and his popcorn lands on the people around him. "Sorry."

"That was wizardry. Pure wizardry," Hall adds.

Meanwhile, Clair Bee is stunned speechless on the side-line.

Hillhouse approaches Hank. "You lucky son of a bitch!"

Hank looks Hillhouse squarely in his beady eyes and moves into position for defense.

"Jules Bender inbounds the ball to Myron Sewitch who passes to Hillhouse near the foul line," Hall says. "But Luisetti snatches it, dribbles once, pivots backward on his right leg, and releases a high hook shot. The ball sails over the extended arms of the giant Hillhouse and... it swishes through the net. Chalk up another two for Luisetti."

Hillhouse, thoroughly finessed, is speechless as Hank stares him down before bolting back to action. The crowd cheers, and Hillhouse looks around at the traitors in the stands.

Howie jogs past Hank. "They love you!"

Clair Bee calls a timeout.

Hank calls his team to him, and he swings his right arm around Dinty and his left around Spook. Everyone else follows suit until the team is entwined in a circle.

"Art, the big guy's going to stick to you like glue. Lure him toward the left wing so we can have some fun in the lane. Let's use their man-to-man against them."

Art nods and Hank nods back.

"Let's jog in using formation two." He claps, and each Indian breaks from the circle following the man to his right like train cars trailing a locomotive. When they approach the center of the court, Hank claps, and they scatter to their positions.

Spook passes Hillhouse and says, "Hi!"

Hillhouse looks at Spook as if he were a leper before matching up with Art.

Hall calls the play. "Dan Kaplowitz inbounds the ball and flips to... Luisetti steals it again! That kid is everywhere! The teams scramble to the basket. Luisetti pitches to Dinty Moore, who passes right back to Luisetti. He dribbles forward, jumps, and shoots. The ball bounces off the rim, but Luisetti rebounds his own ball, pumps, spins in the air, and stuffs it through the net! Oh, my word! He jumped higher than the hoop and just pushed it through. Why on earth was Hillhouse off in the corner with Stoefen?"

The Garden explodes in a deafening cheer, and Clair Bee slams his clipboard into the floor. Myron Sewitch inbounds to Jules. Hank picks him up and traps him in a corner. Spook comes from behind Jules and smacks it free. Hank grabs the ball and dribbles away leaving Jules behind. Hank gets picked up by Irving who uses the time-honored technique of placing a hand on the offensive player, but Hank pushes it off. A whistle halts the action.

"Luisetti gets called for his first foul of the game," Hall says. "And he's jogging toward the ref."

Just feet from the official, Hank stops and says, "May I ask you a question?"

The ref looks at Hank with curiosity.

"If he has a hand on me on offense, am I allowed to put my hand on him?"

"What do you mean, son?"

"Can I keep my arm out to keep his hand off of me?"

"That's okay as long as you don't hold him."

As Hank walks away, Hall adds, "Luisetti and the ref finish their powwow, and the action continues. Kaplowitz inbounds to Myron Sewitch. He dribbles to the left corner where he's doubled up by Dinty Moore and Spook Calderwood. Sewitch passes to Kaplowitz, who shoots and misses. Luisetti grabs the rebound over Hillhouse and shovels off to Spook Calderwood. He dribbles through a flurry of players and passes back to Luisetti, covered by Jules Bender at the top of the key. Luisetti moves right, stops, and locks eyes with Bender. Luisetti rocks in a stationary position, dribbling the ball through his legs and around his body in a show of athleticism like I've never seen. He bursts by Bender and drives toward the basket. Hillhouse leaves Stoefen and runs at Luisetti. They leap together. Luisetti fakes a shot but fires to Stoefen who shoots a one-hander and nails it! The Blackbird lead is in jeopardy for the first time! Ladies and Gentlemen, we are witnessing basketball history!"

Stefano cheers.

Amalia looks at Ricky and smiles.

Eddie fists Mario's shirt and shakes him.

The Stanford bench cheers.

Clair Bee frantically signals time. His dreary, sweaty team gathers around him. He snaps orders, points at them, and makes exaggerated hand motions.

A whistle blows and the action continues.

Jules misses.

Spook scores.

Art scores.

Dinty scores.

And Hank is everywhere. Every point Stanford makes is either Hank's goal or his assist. He is everywhere the ball is.

"Art Stoefen launches a one-arm pass to Luisetti who's racing toward the basket," Hall cries into the mic. "He hauls it in like a center fielder snagging a ball overhead. Luisetti takes two, long, jumping steps, and leaps, legs spread. Oh, Sweet Jesus. He's nearly flying through the air! The ball rolls off his fingers and through the net. If I didn't see that with my own eyes, I wouldn't believe it. In fact, I still don't know if I believe it!"

The crowd erupts like a volcano. Paper cups and rolls of

toilet paper rain down like a ticker-tape parade. Wally lets fly with another load of popcorn.

Bradford scribbles on his pad.

Parks pops off another photo.

A lifeless Clair Bee looks up at the scoreboard that shows the fourth quarter tally in neon letters: LIU 32, Stanford 48.

The cartoonist draws a picture of Hank high in the air, legs spread apart, with the ball just about to fall in. He scribbles: 'Look Mom, he can fly' in a caption above a boy standing and pointing at Hank.

Kilpatrick playfully punches Nat Holman in the arm. "That kid's a star! I've never seen anyone do more things with a ball!"

Holman looks ill and rubs his arm when no one is looking.

Irish takes a drag of his cigarette, eyes the fans, and smiles.

Hank, guarded by Irving, uses his arm to keep him from touching him.

Clair Bee cups his hands around his mouth and shouts, "That's holding! Holding! Are you blind?"

The ref points at Bee. "Are you telling me how to do my job or are you saying I'm incompetent? Knock it off, Clair!"

Hank drives, stops, leaps, and passes behind his back to Howie. He flips it to Spook, who shoots and scores. Irving inbounds and shoots it to Hillhouse, who leads Jules with a monster pass.

Hall grabs the microphone. "Jules Bender dribbles with Luisetti in pursuit. Bender goes in for the layup, but Luisetti stuffs it and retrieves the ball. Luisetti pitches it to Moore, who fakes a shot, then rushes the lane, shoots, and scores! With Stoefen dragging Hillhouse in the corner, Stanford is having a party in there."

Hank hooks a thirty-footer without even looking at the basket.

Hank hits one with his right arm.

Hank sinks one with his left arm.

A sweaty, trodden Hillhouse puts his hand on Jules' shoulder. Jules is bent over with his hands on his knees.

With one minute remaining in the fourth quarter, the scoreboard reads: LIU 44, Stanford 70.

"While every one of these California kids fire away with lethal one-handed shots that are impossible to stop, I have never seen anything like Luisetti," Hall says. "After tonight, basketball will never be the same again."

Stefano shakes Ricky's hand. "Thank-a you so much!"

The crowd chants the final five seconds as Hank, with the bandage now crimson, dribbles the ball low to the ground, threading his way toward the basket. He looks left, right, then shoots a high forty-foot one-hander and spears it straight through the eye of the basket.

The buzzer sounds, and the crowd lets loose like the hammers of hell.

Bradford cheers and Parks snaps a picture.

The Stanford players mob Luisetti as they run to the sideline and join the rest of the team.

John Bunn embraces Hank. "You are the best I've ever seen—maybe the best they'll ever be!"

The LIU players and Clair Bee stand together, desolate and beaten.

Spook grabs Wally's hand and leads him over to Hank. The boy looks at his hero with awe and hugs him tightly around the waist. Hank pats his back. Wally breaks away and beckons Hank to crouch down for a secret.

MADNESS

"I'll never forget you, Hank Luisetti. I'm going to play basketball and tell everyone I know about you."

Eric Parks snaps a picture of Hank and Wally shaking hands just as they part. Parks kneels next to Wally and says, "How would you like that picture, son?"

"I sure would!"

"So would I," Hank says.

"You got it!"

Stefano, Amalia, Ricky, Eddie, and the rest of the Galileo crew join Hank on the sideline, and each takes a turn hugging him as the crowd chants his name.

John Bunn taps his star forward on the shoulder. "I hate to interrupt, but you'd better take a bow before a riot breaks out."

Hank jogs onto the court and waves in all directions.

Jules claps. Hillhouse follows suit along with Clair and the rest of the Blackbirds.

A standing ovation begins. Ned Irish, Brian Hurley, and Kilpatrick all stand. Ned Irish eyes Nat Holman until he gets to his feet. Irish continues looking until Holman claps.

A police officer approaches the Stanford sideline and speaks to the group. Dinty snaps his head in a double take and nods with quick bobs of his head. The officer points behind him, and Dinty rockets in that direction, nearly knocking down those applauding Hank who've spilled onto the perimeter of the court. When Dinty clears a few hurdles of people, he sees Connie with her father waiting with another police officer at the sideline entrance. He gives her a quick hug and leads her onto the court floor. Connie freezes when she sees Hank standing center, waving to the crowd with a bloody bandage over his eye. Tears stream down her cheeks. Dinty jogs to Hank, calling his name. He turns and Dinty points to

Connie.

Hank sprints over and picks her up off the floor, hugging her in circles. The audience loves it, and the cheers swell. He puts her down and asks her something. She points to her father, who waves, and he waves back. Hank picks her up again, and the two kiss passionately — alone in the midst of nearly 18,000 cheering people. Connie's engagement ring is absent from her left hand.

EPILOGUE

"The Stanford-LIU game was no mere intersectional upset. It was a pivotal game in the sport's history, introducing the nation to modern basketball. Players throughout the country began shooting on the run and with one hand. The deliberate style of play would give way to the fast break, the man-to-man would yield to the zone and combination defenses, and the following season, the center jump after goals would be abandoned forever. Scoring suddenly increased, and a game that had served, in many areas, merely to fill the gap between baseball and football seasons, abruptly began to enjoy widespread popularity on its own. For anything big to happen then, it had to happen in New York. Luisetti and the Laughing Boys happened there in the winter of 1936."

By Ron Fimrite
Sports Illustrated

Hank was named the most outstanding athlete to perform in Madison Square Garden in 1936, and the following season, Stanford beat LIU and CCNY in consecutive nights.

Hank set college scoring records every year he played. After graduation, Luisetti played himself in the film, Campus Confessions, staring Betty Grable. While serving in World War II, Hank contracted spinal meningitis and barely survived the illness. The sulfa drugs used to treat him damaged his heart, and he could no longer play competitive basketball. He turned down lucrative offers from several teams when the

NBA formed in 1946.

Stanford retired Hank's number seven jersey, and in 1987, teammate Phil Zonne created an on-campus bronze statue of Luisetti shooting his famous one-hander, which still stands today.

Hank Luisetti died in December of 2002 at the age of eighty-six. He is survived by a son, daughter, and several grandchildren and great-grandchildren.

A Note from the Author

I would like to thank you for purchasing Madness. As an up-coming author, it is valuable to receive Amazon book reviews. Just go to https://getbook.at/madnesskindle, click the book, and scroll down to "review this book." Every single one is greatly appreciated.

MY CONTACT INFO:

greentbooks@gmail.com
https://twitter.com/mdeluciabooks

I will reply to every message I receive, so please contact me if...

- You would like me to do a book talk or signing

- You have a question about writing or about the book

- You'd like to be on my mailing list

- You are a teacher or school administrator and would like a review copy to be considered as a curriculum read or to be put on summer or outside reading lists. You will get a free copy if you contact me using your school email.

If you enjoyed this book, you would also like my short story Settling A Score. Set in the Bronx during the 1960s, Settling A

Score tells the story of two estranged brothers, Mark and Louis, who are accidentally placed on the same little league team. Over the course of the season, they learn about life, each other, and the enduring challenges of being brothers.

Amazon Reviews:

"Wanted more. I felt for the kid. It was a terrific story. I couldn't stop reading it."

"I read this author's other two books, so I thought I'd give this one a read. I think I'm officially a fan of this guy."

About the Author

Mike DeLucia grew up in the Throggs Neck/Pelham Bay section of the Bronx and spent his childhood playing baseball, softball, basketball and all of the street games associated with city living in the '60s and '70s. He began his career as an actor and entrepreneur but wound up teaching high school English in his forties. Besides Madness, Mike has published Boycott the Yankees: A Call to Action by a Lifelong Yankees Fan, and Settling A Score, a short story. He travels the world with his wife, Lillian, and has two children and one grandchild

www.booksbymikedelucia.com